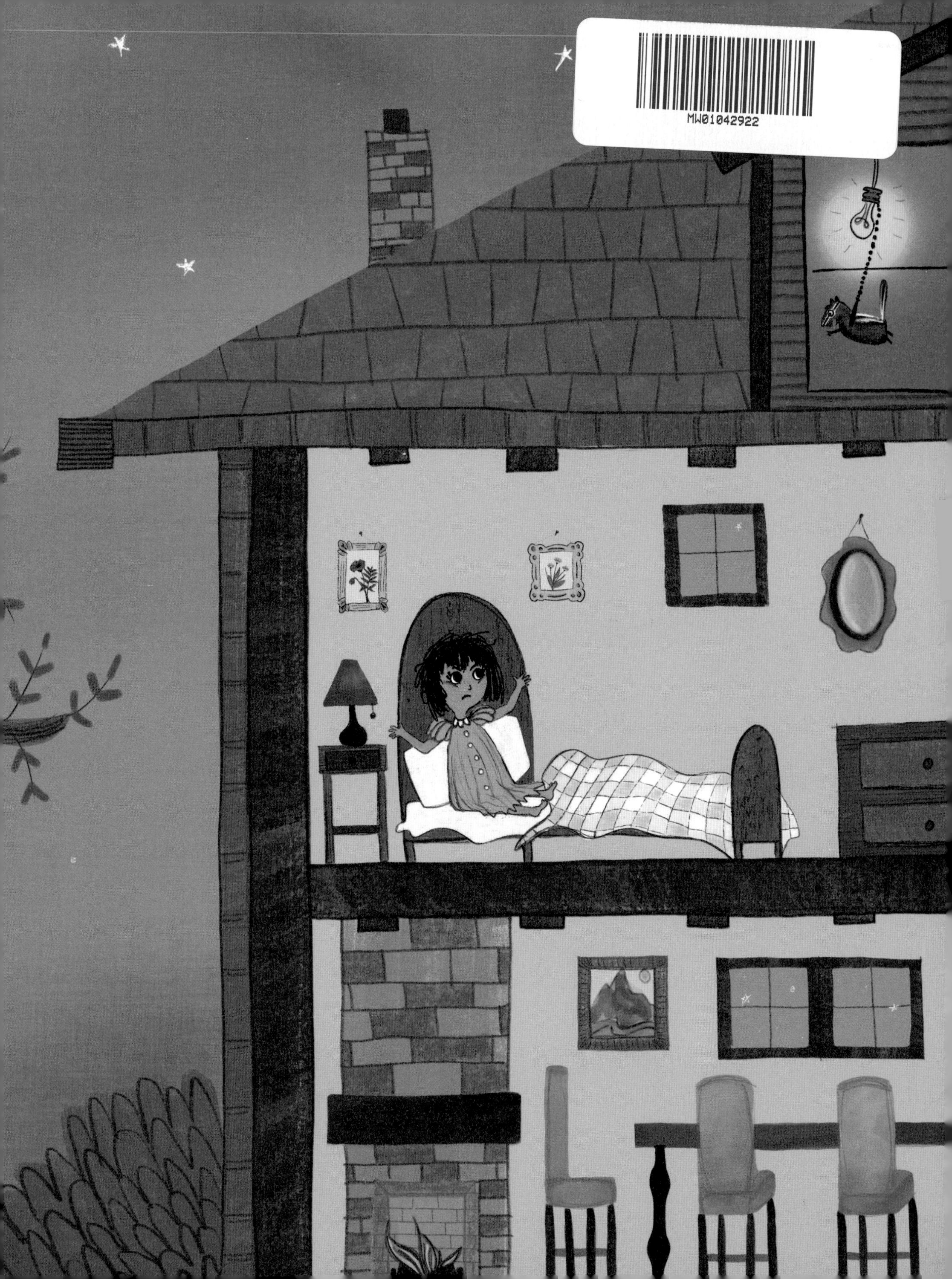

For my nieces and nephews, your flourishing
minds inspire me.
 - Jacqueline Leigh

For Hank, with love, always. YOU are
my masterpiece.
 - Erika Wilson

Eva & Lincoln,
Enjoy Life &
always Choose
Fun!
Jacqueline
Leigh

MASCOT® BOOKS

www.mascotbooks.com

Skedaddle!

©2020 Jackie Boeheim. All Rights Reserved. No part
of this publication may be reproduced, stored in a
retrieval system or transmitted in any form by any means
electronic, mechanical, or photocopying, recording or
otherwise without the permission of the author.

For more information, please contact:
Mascot Books
620 Herndon Parkway, Suite 320
Herndon, VA 20170
info@mascotbooks.com

Library of Congress Control Number: 2020906072

CPSIA Code: PRT0420A
ISBN-13: 978-1-64543-200-5

Printed in the United States

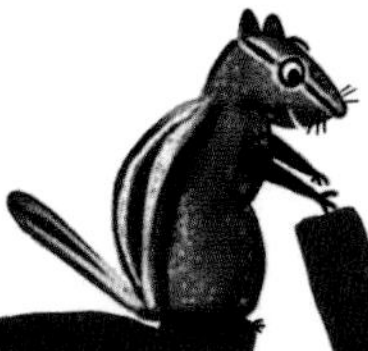

Skedaddle!

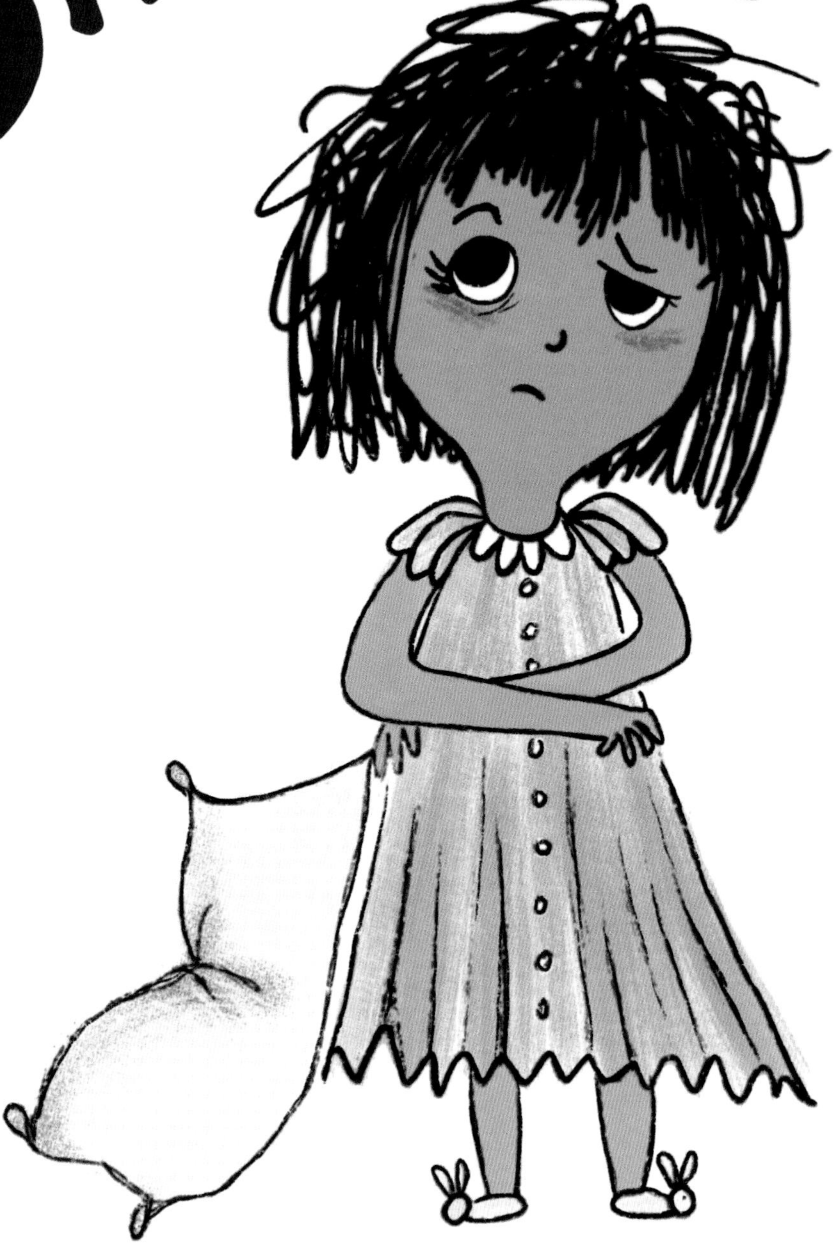

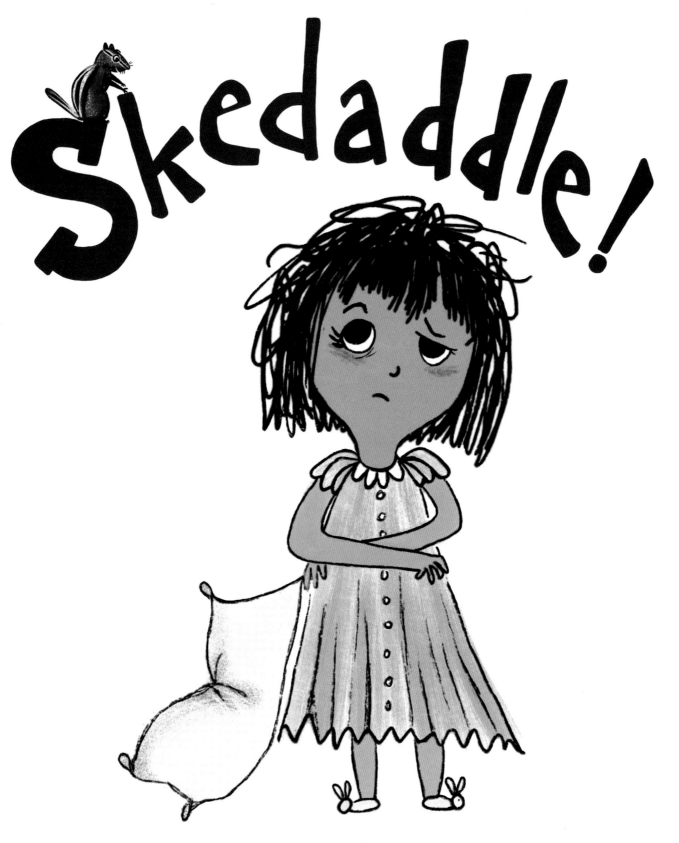

Jacqueline Leigh
Illustrated by Erika Wilson

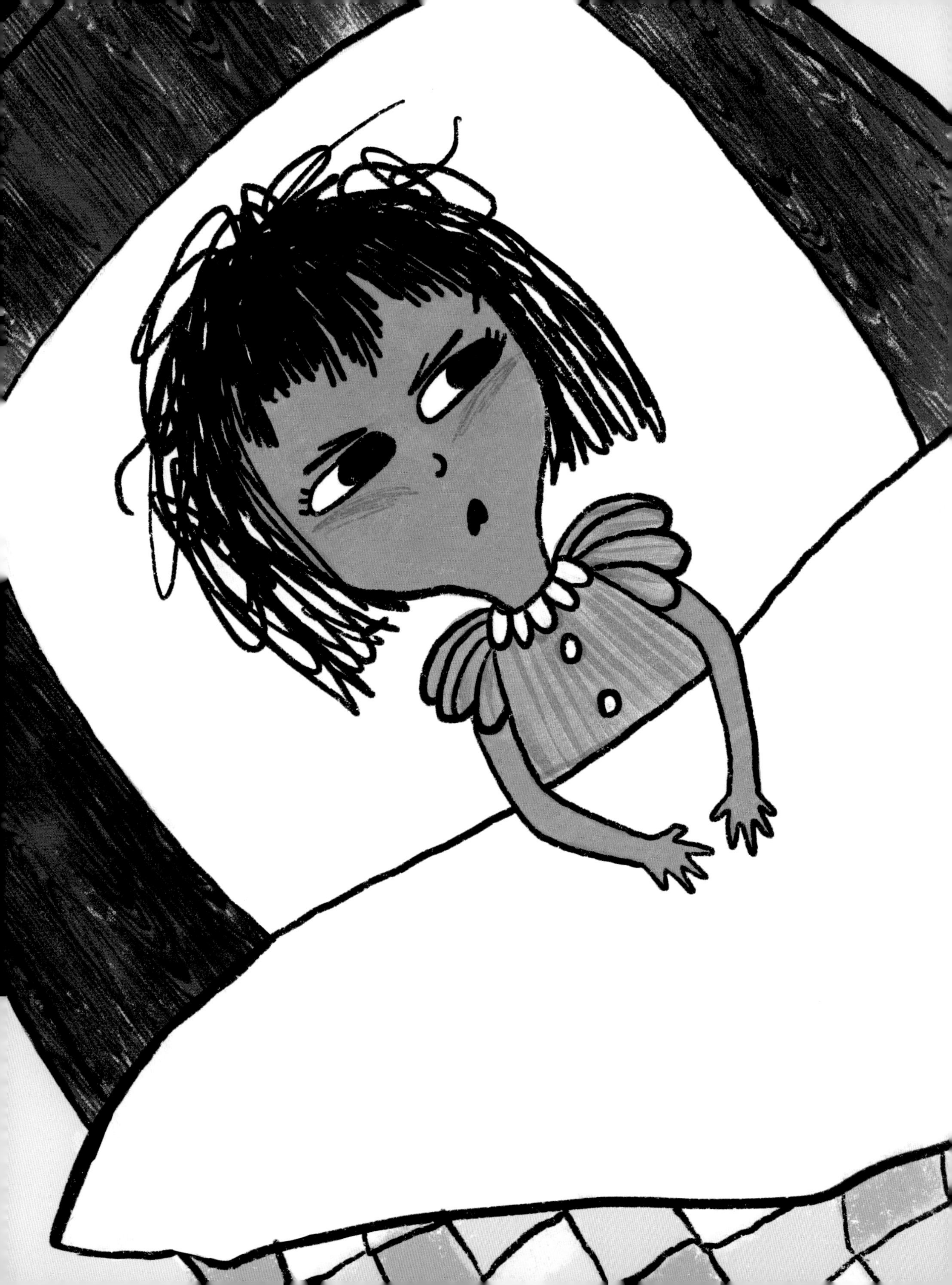

One night, Nellie hears a strange noise above her head.

CHIRRUP, SCRATCH, SQUEAK!

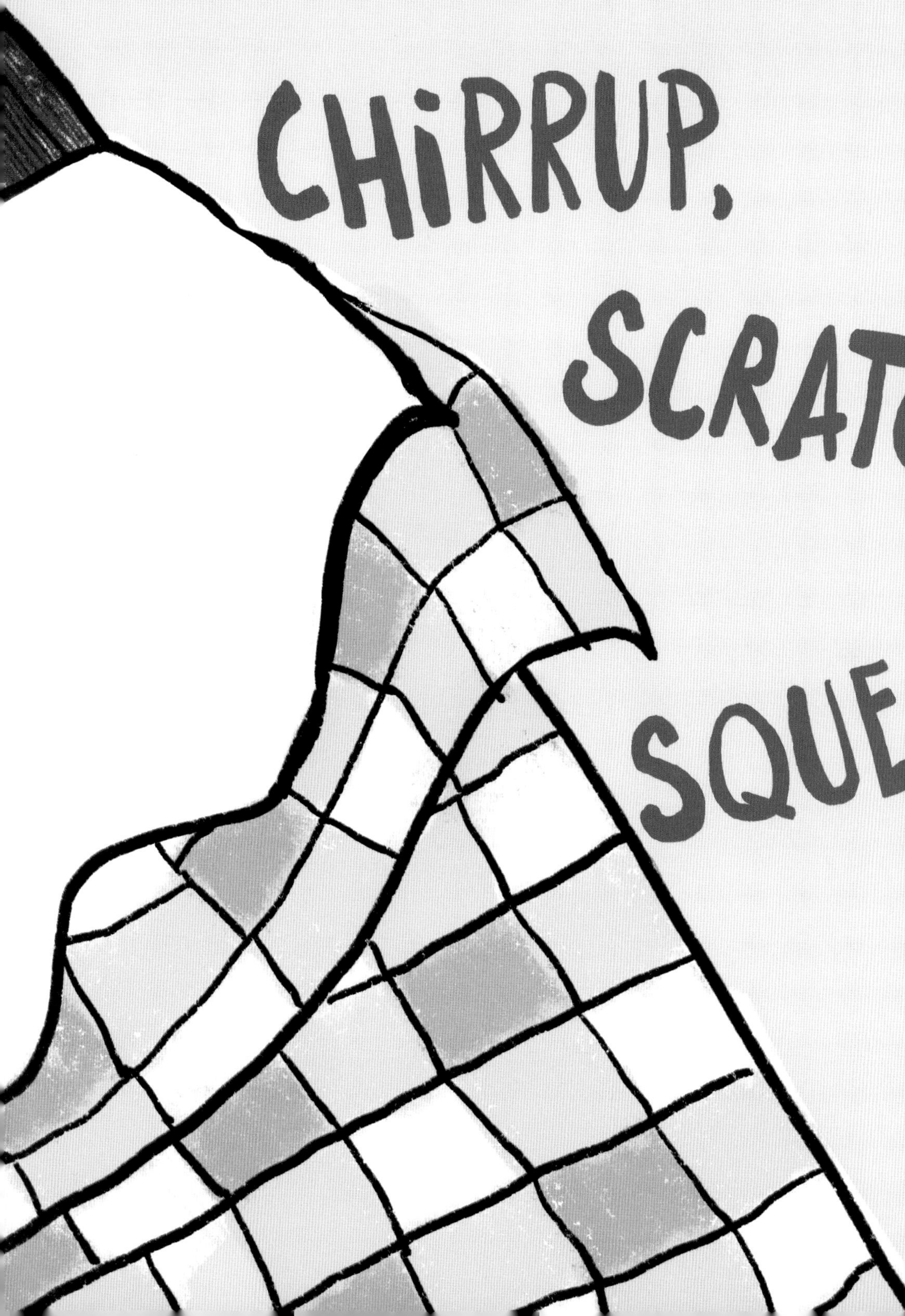

Nellie sits up in bed. What could that be?

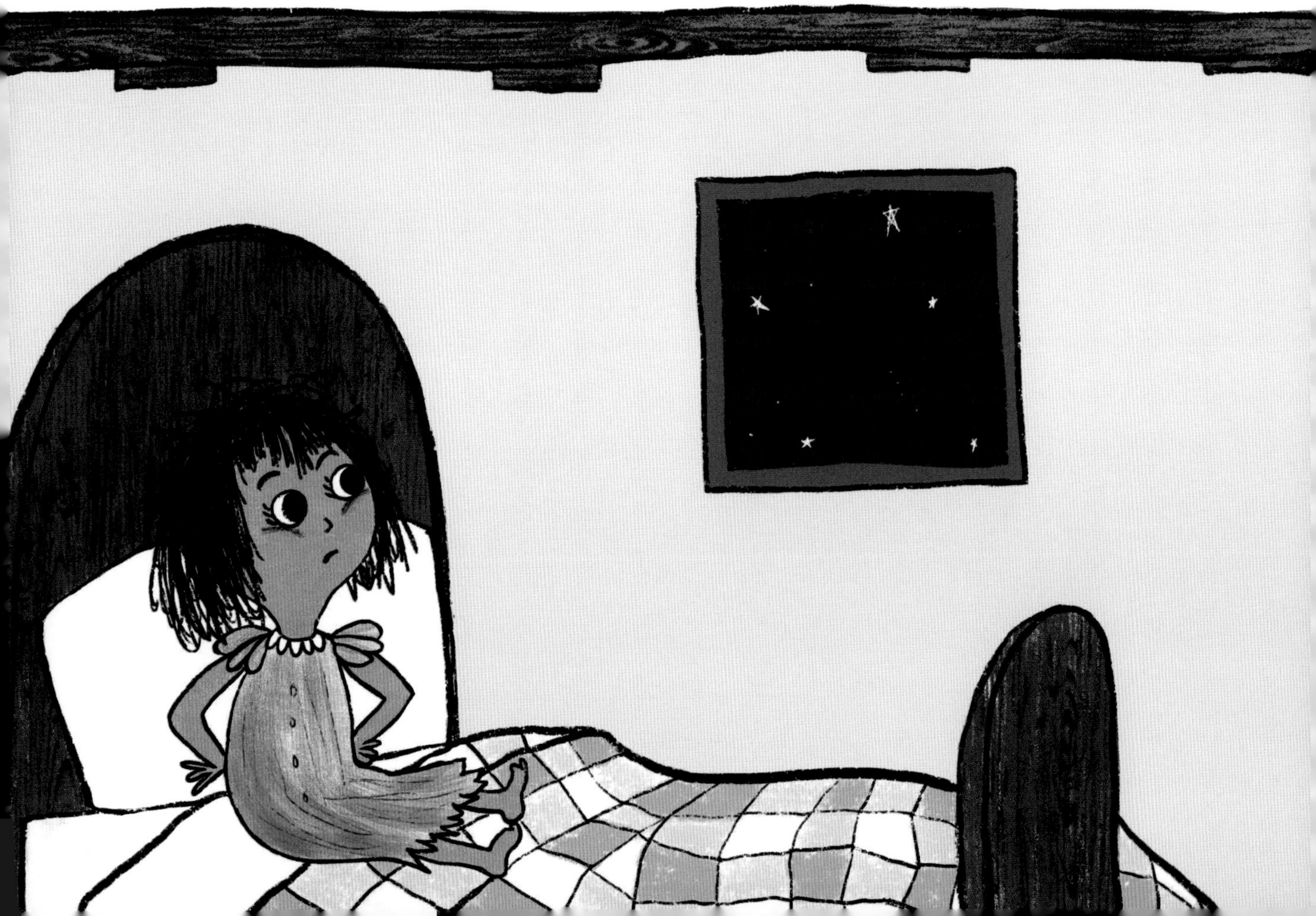

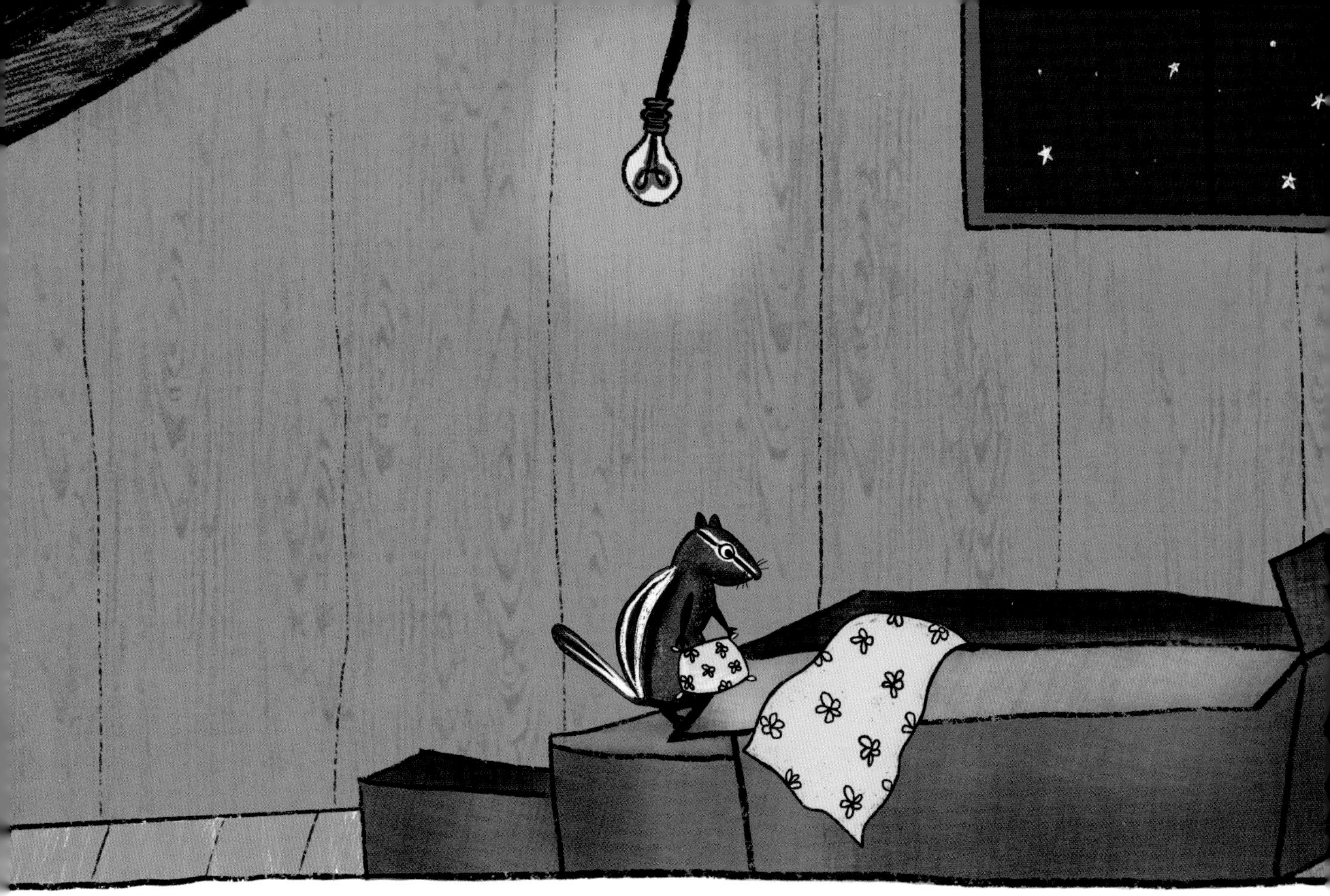

A chipmunk, that's what. He's made himself a cozy home in Nellie's attic.

Nellie lies back down,

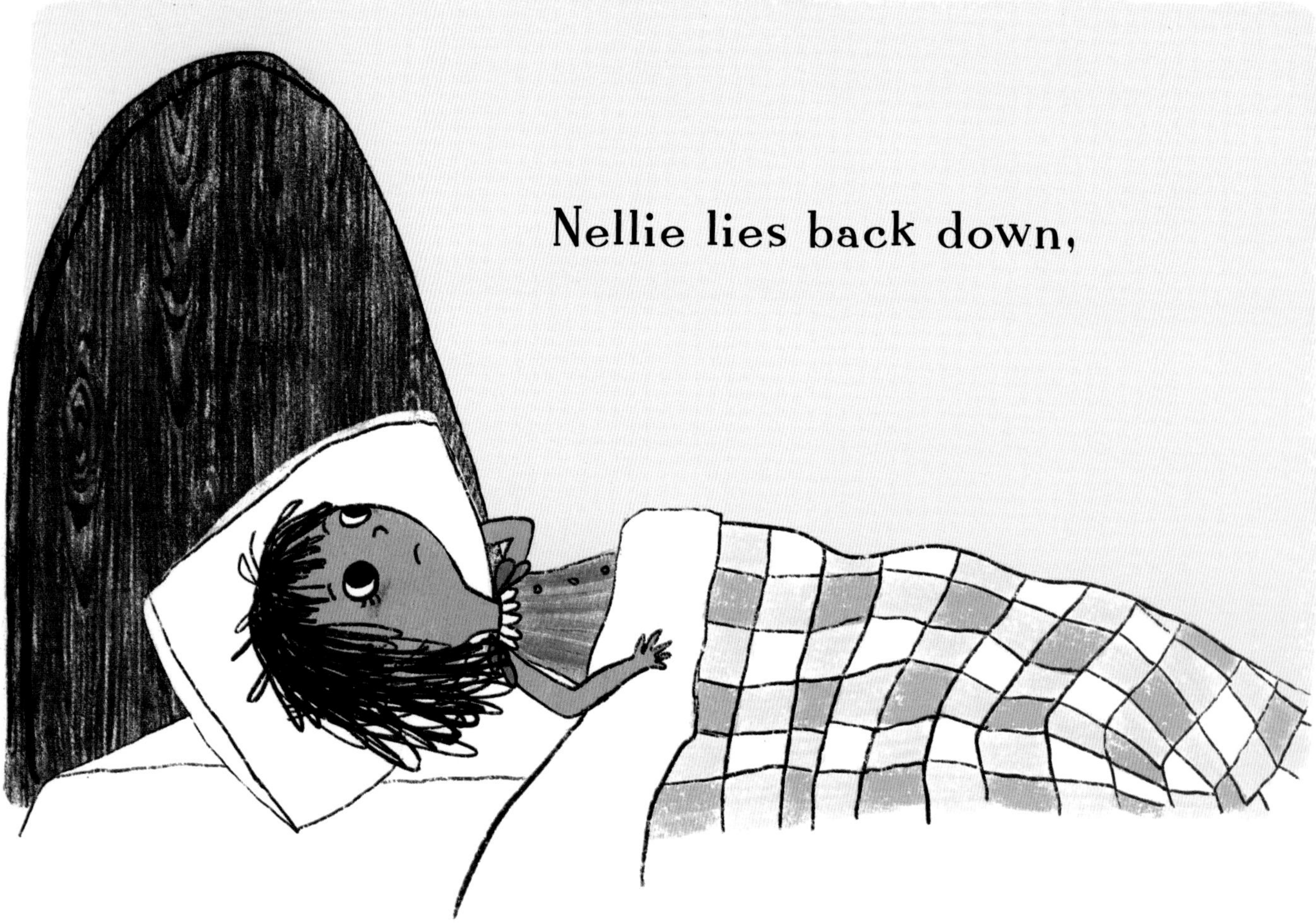

squeezes her eyes tight,

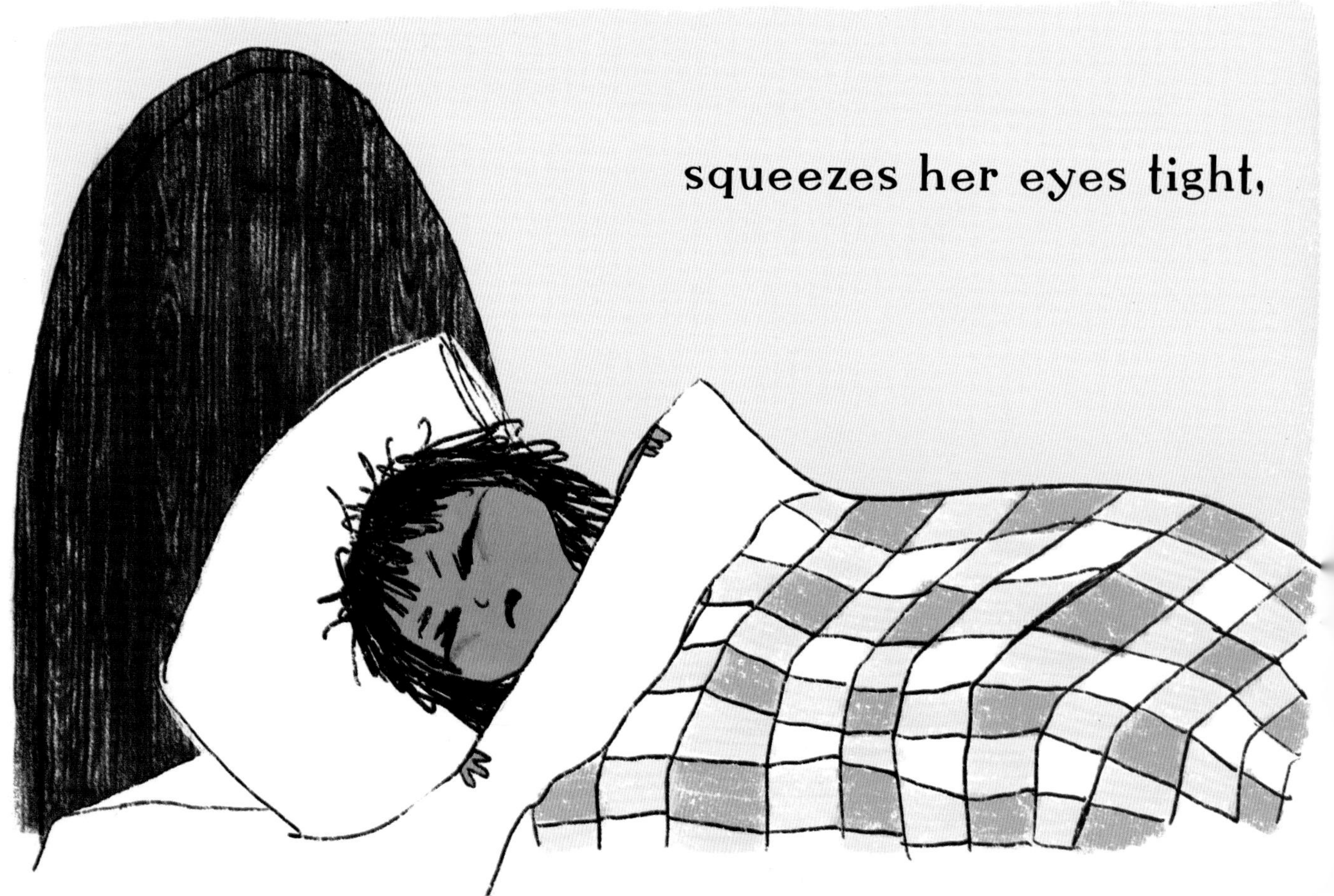

and pulls the covers over her head.

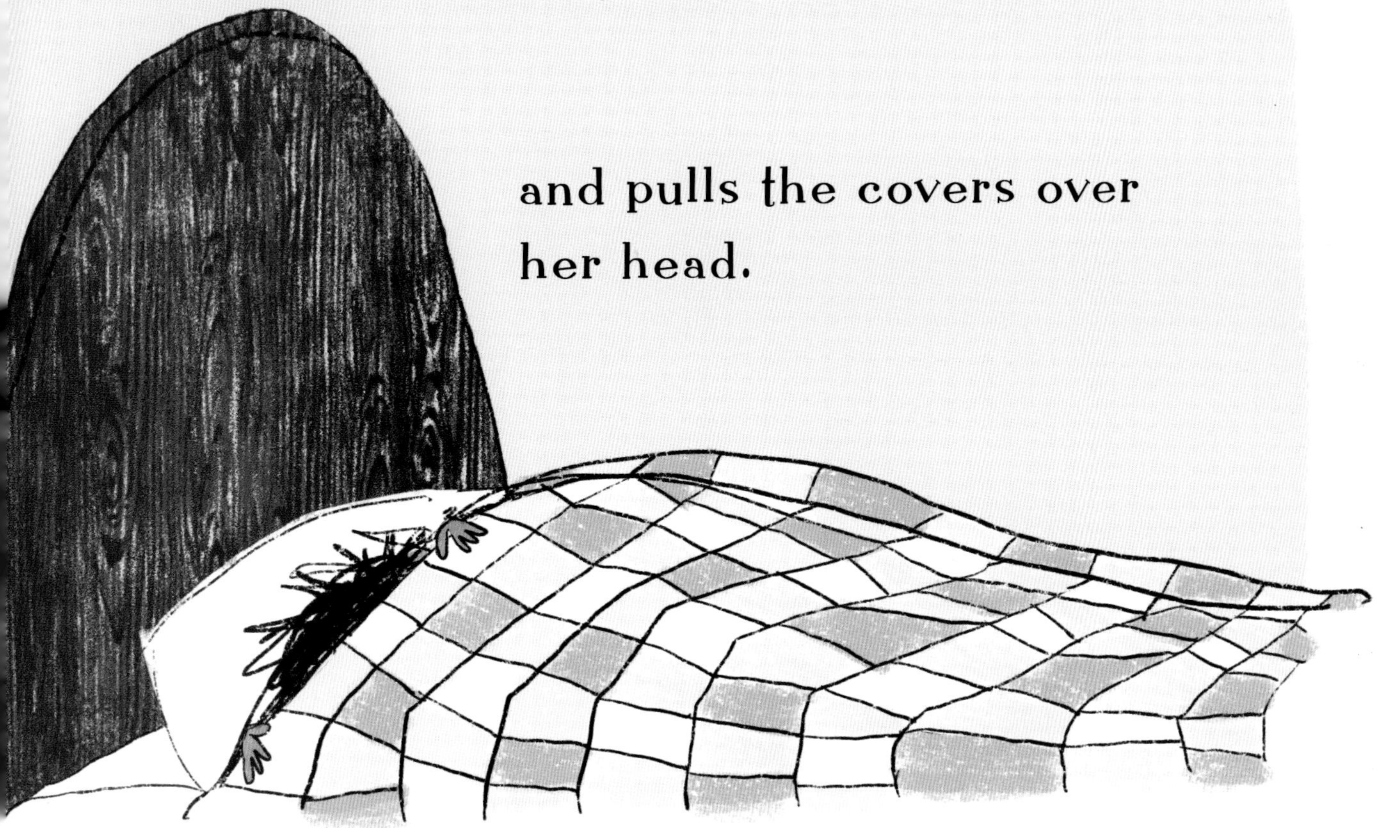

But she can still hear it.

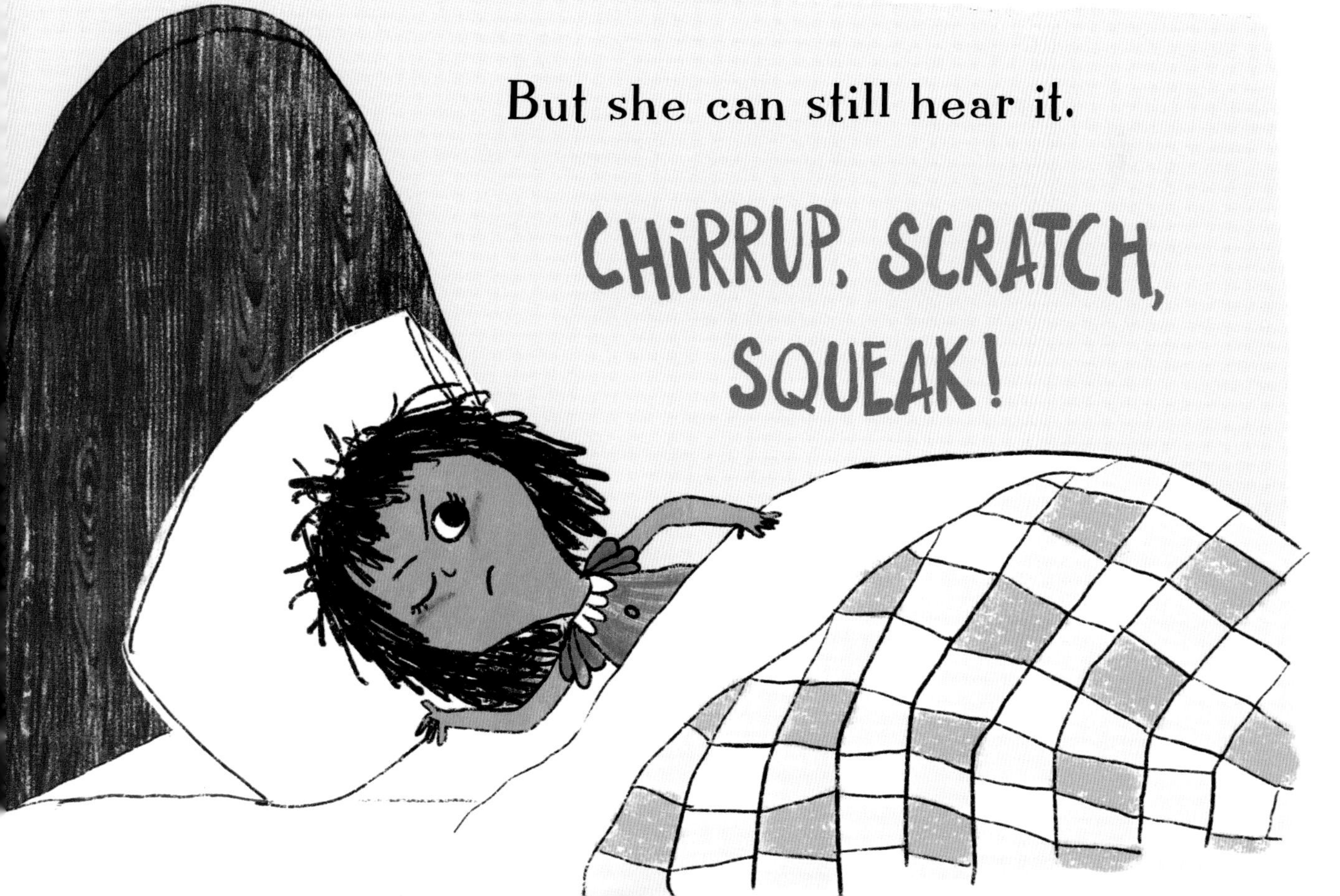
CHIRRUP, SCRATCH,
SQUEAK!

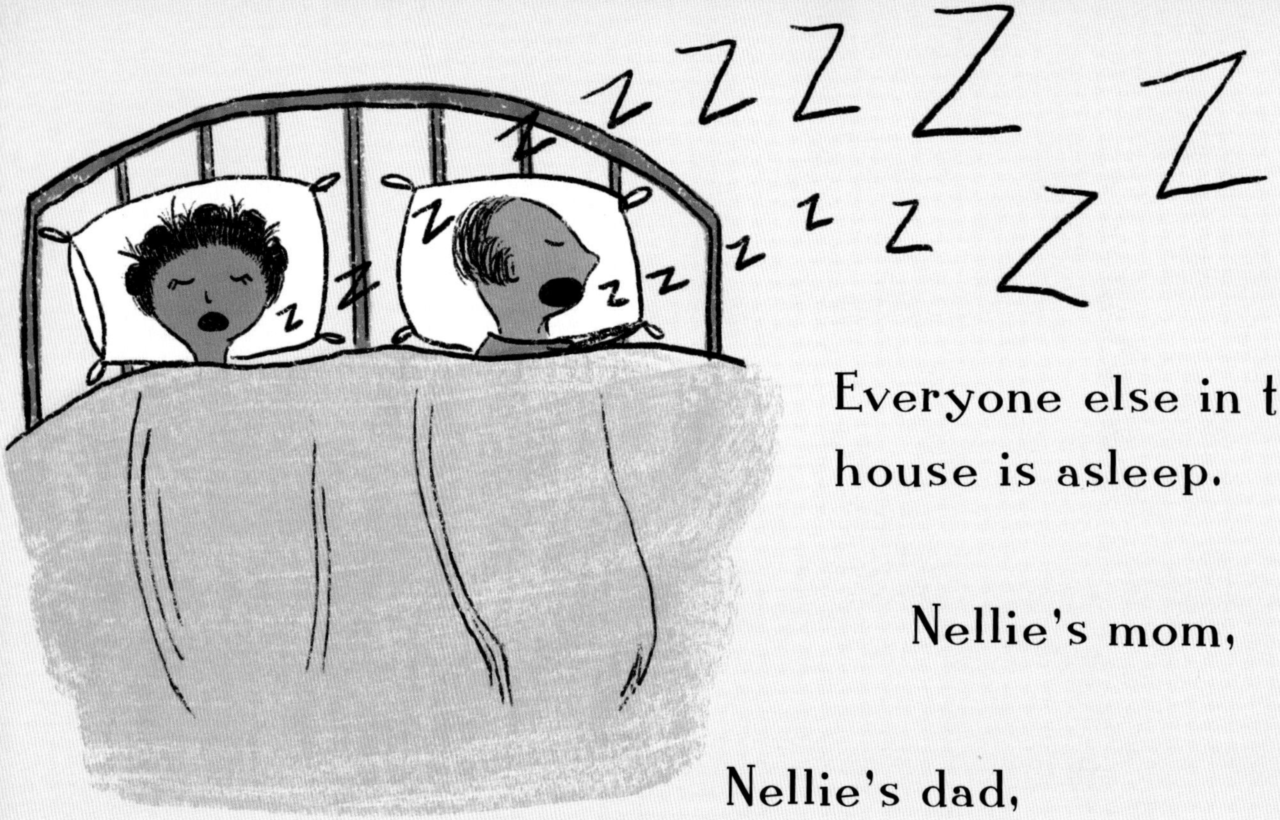

Everyone else in the house is asleep.

Nellie's mom,

Nellie's dad,

and Nellie's cat, Ziggy.

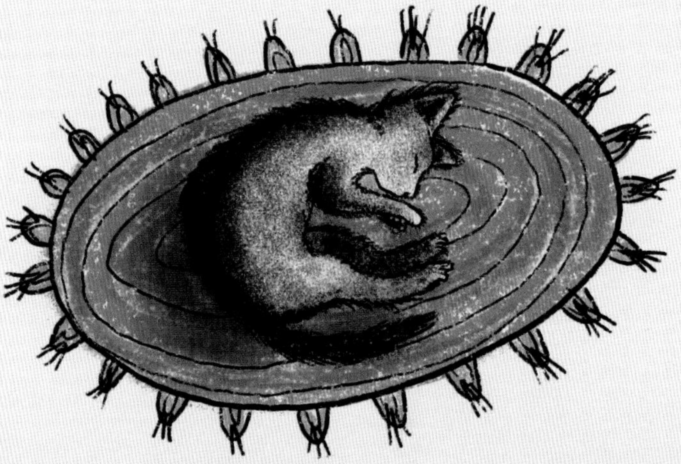

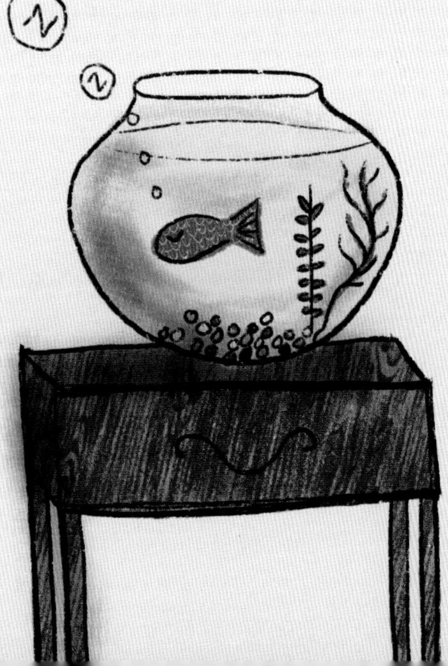

Even Nellie's goldfish is asleep.

But not Nellie.

Because all Nellie can hear is

CHiRRUP, SCRATCH, SQUEAK!

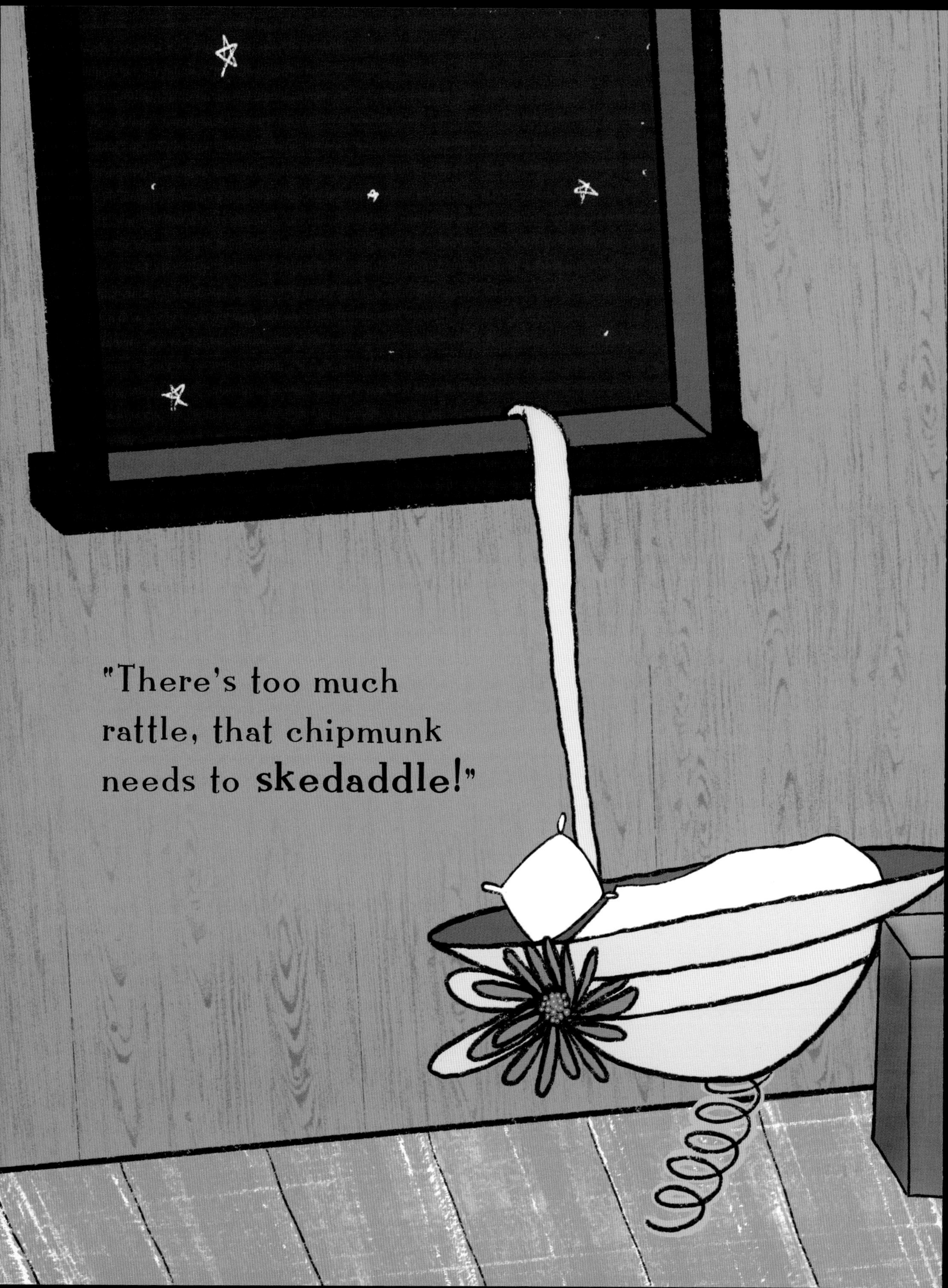

"There's too much rattle, that chipmunk needs to **skedaddle!**"

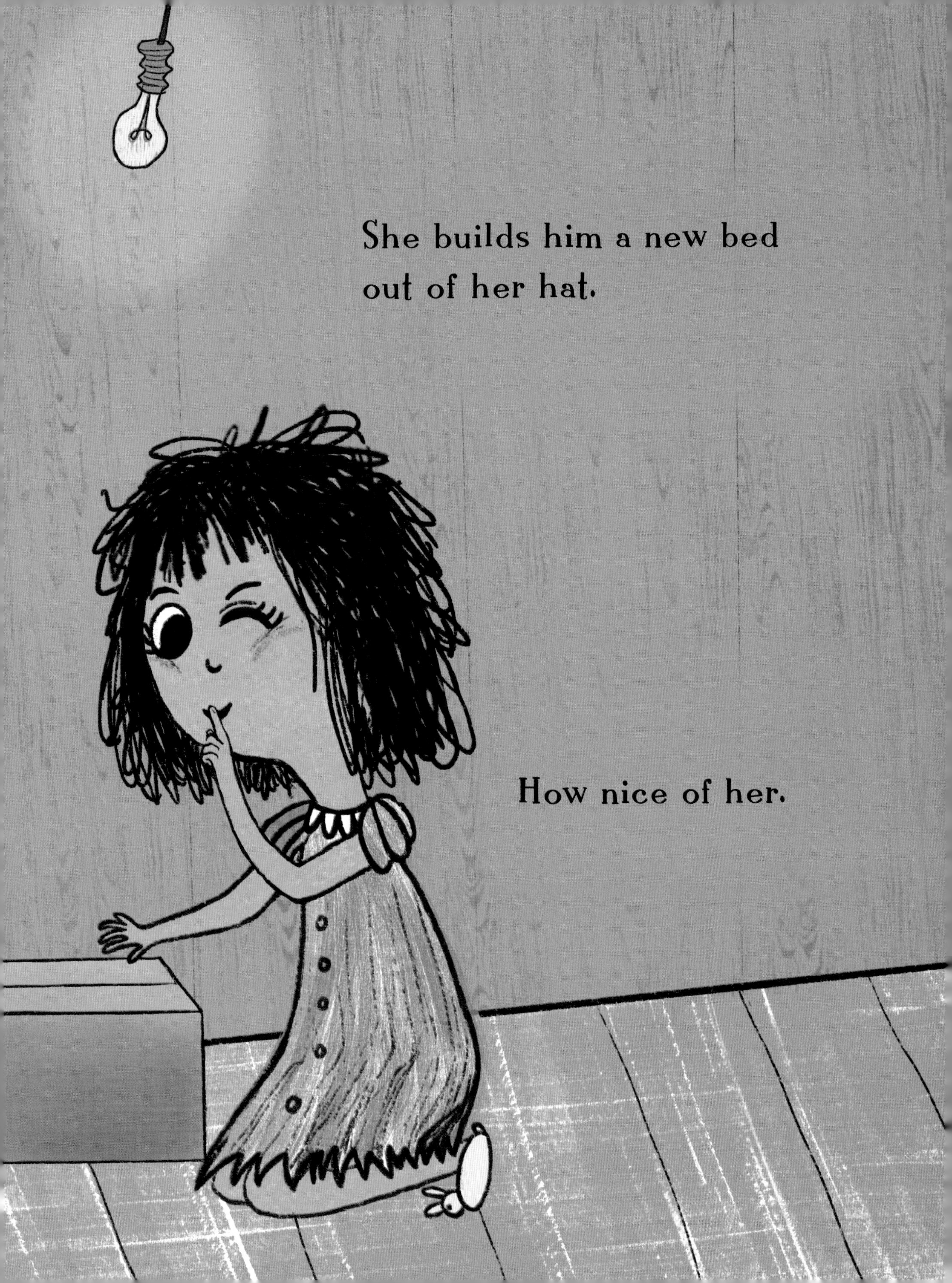

She builds him a new bed
out of her hat.

How nice of her.

Nellie smooths her nightgown,

tucks in her sheet,

and lets out a loud yawn.

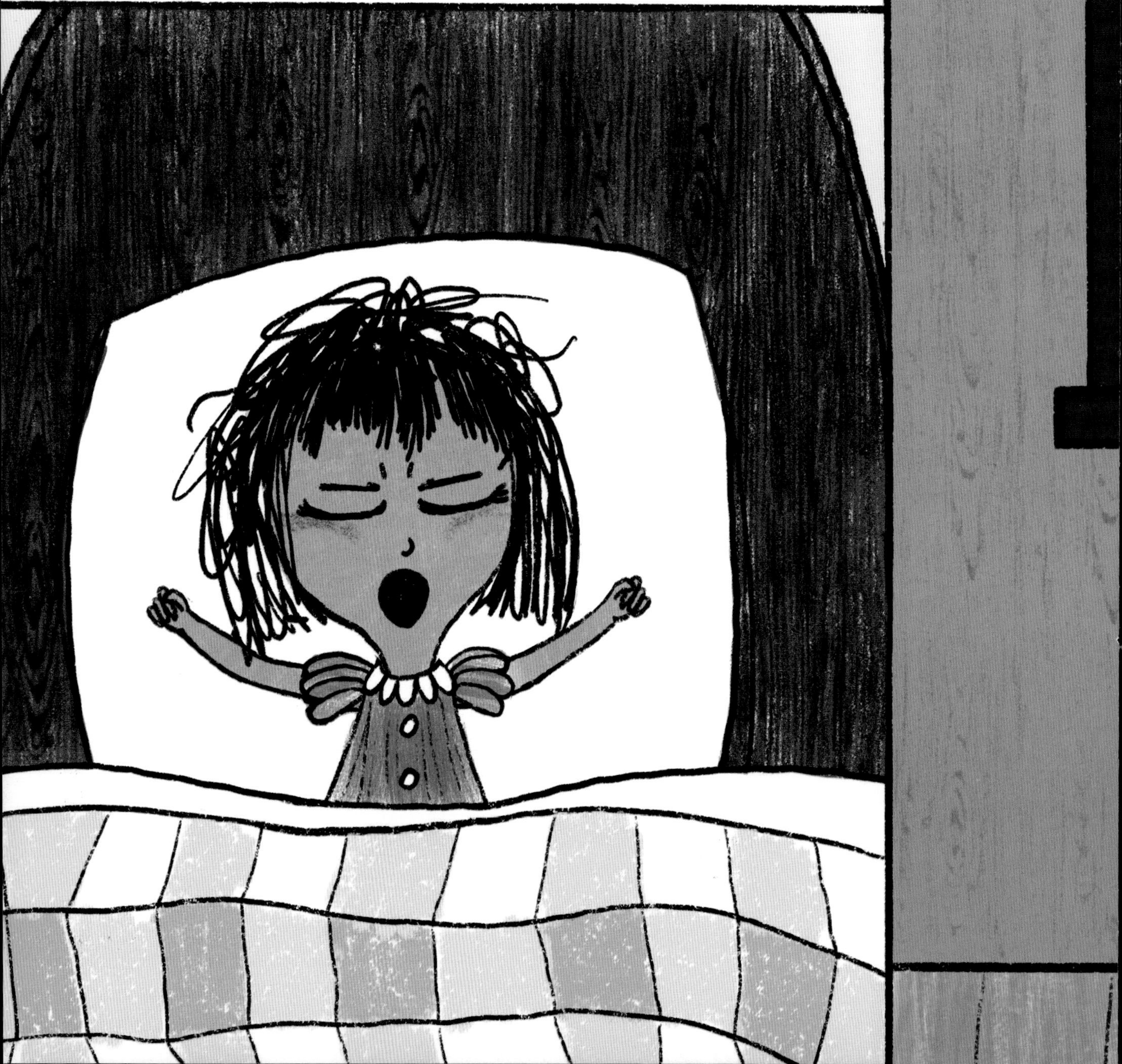

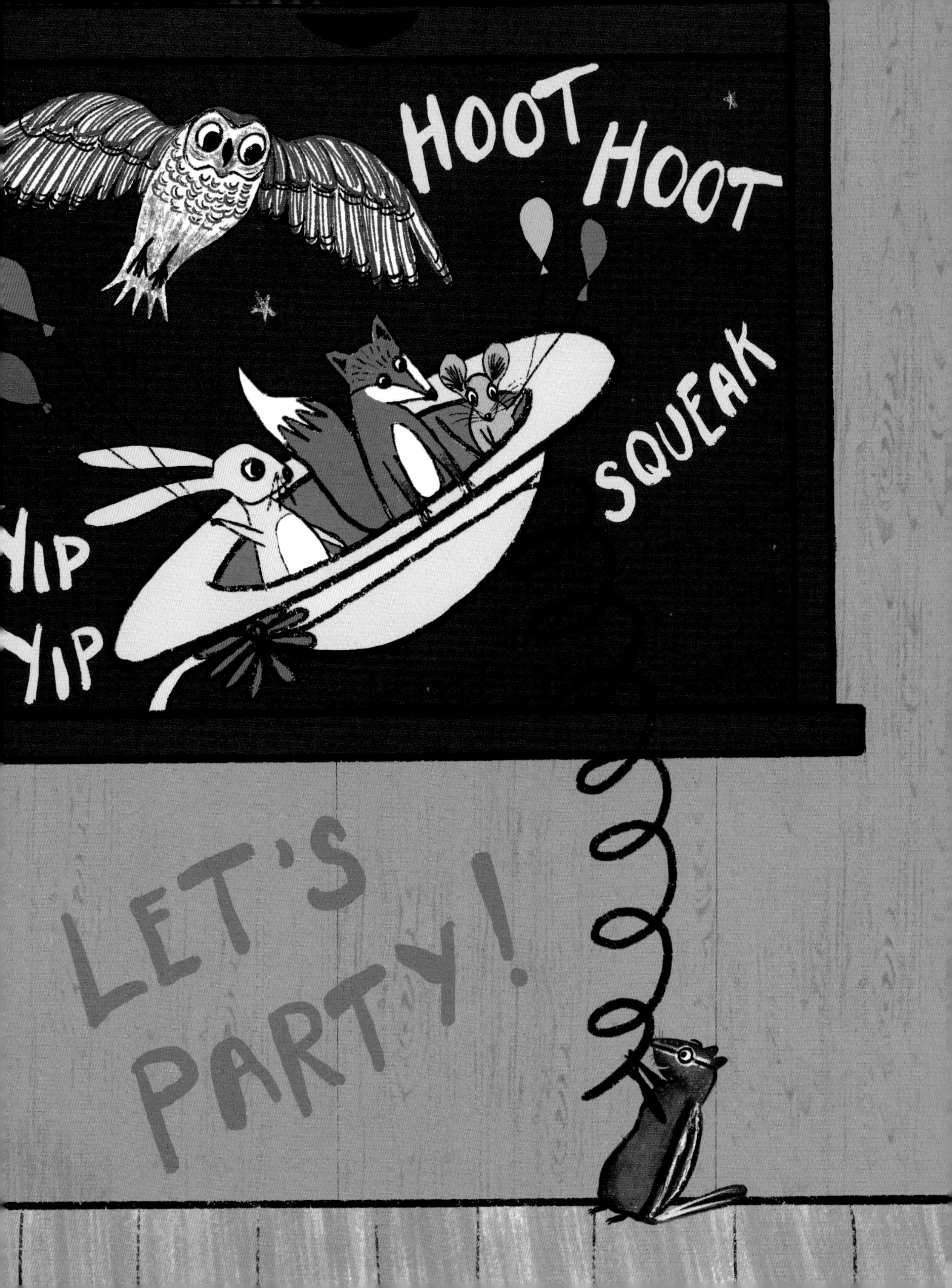
HOOT HOOT
SQUEAK
YIP YIP
LET'S PARTY!

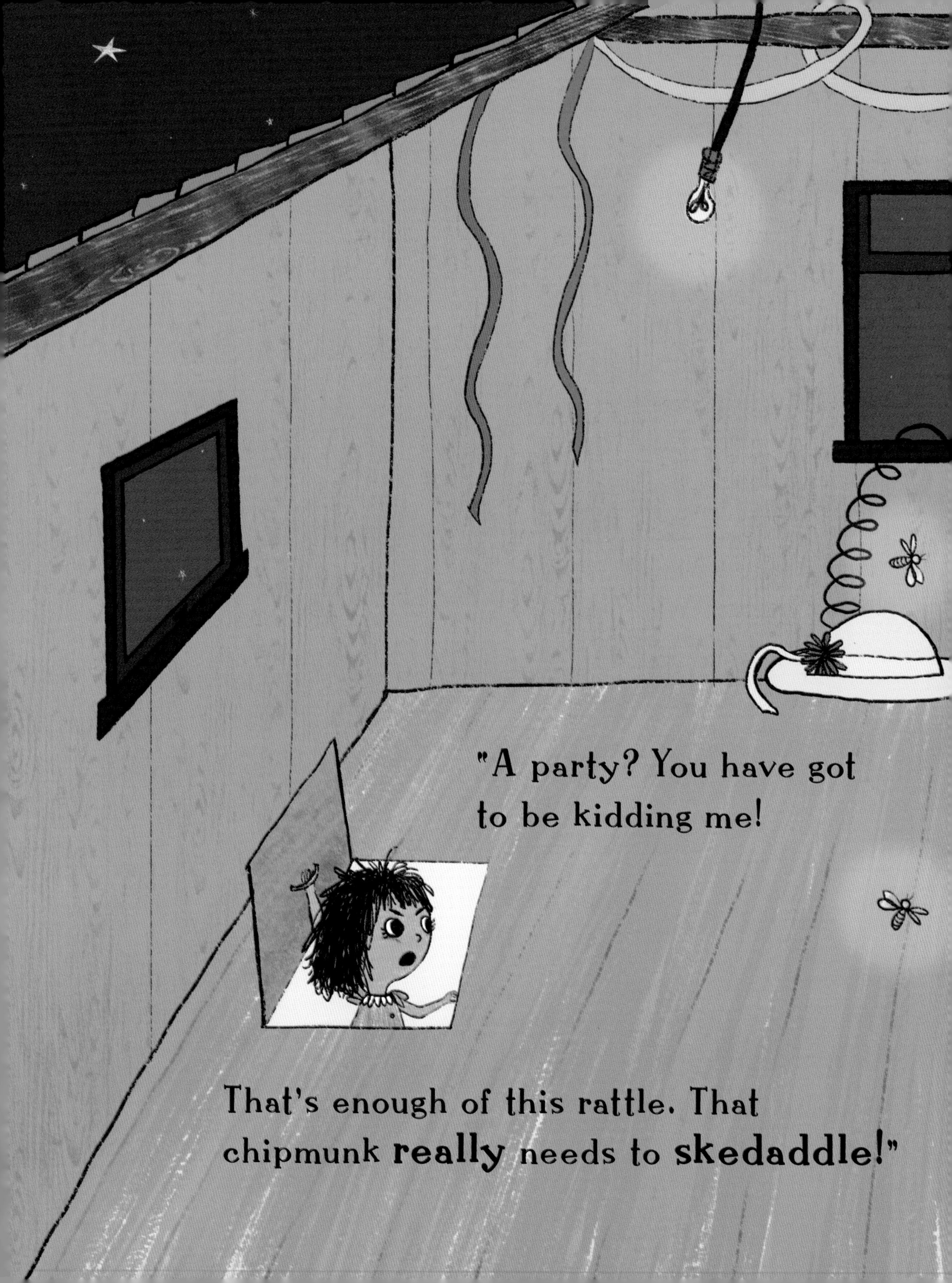

"A party? You have got
to be kidding me!

That's enough of this rattle. That
chipmunk **really** needs to **skedaddle**!"

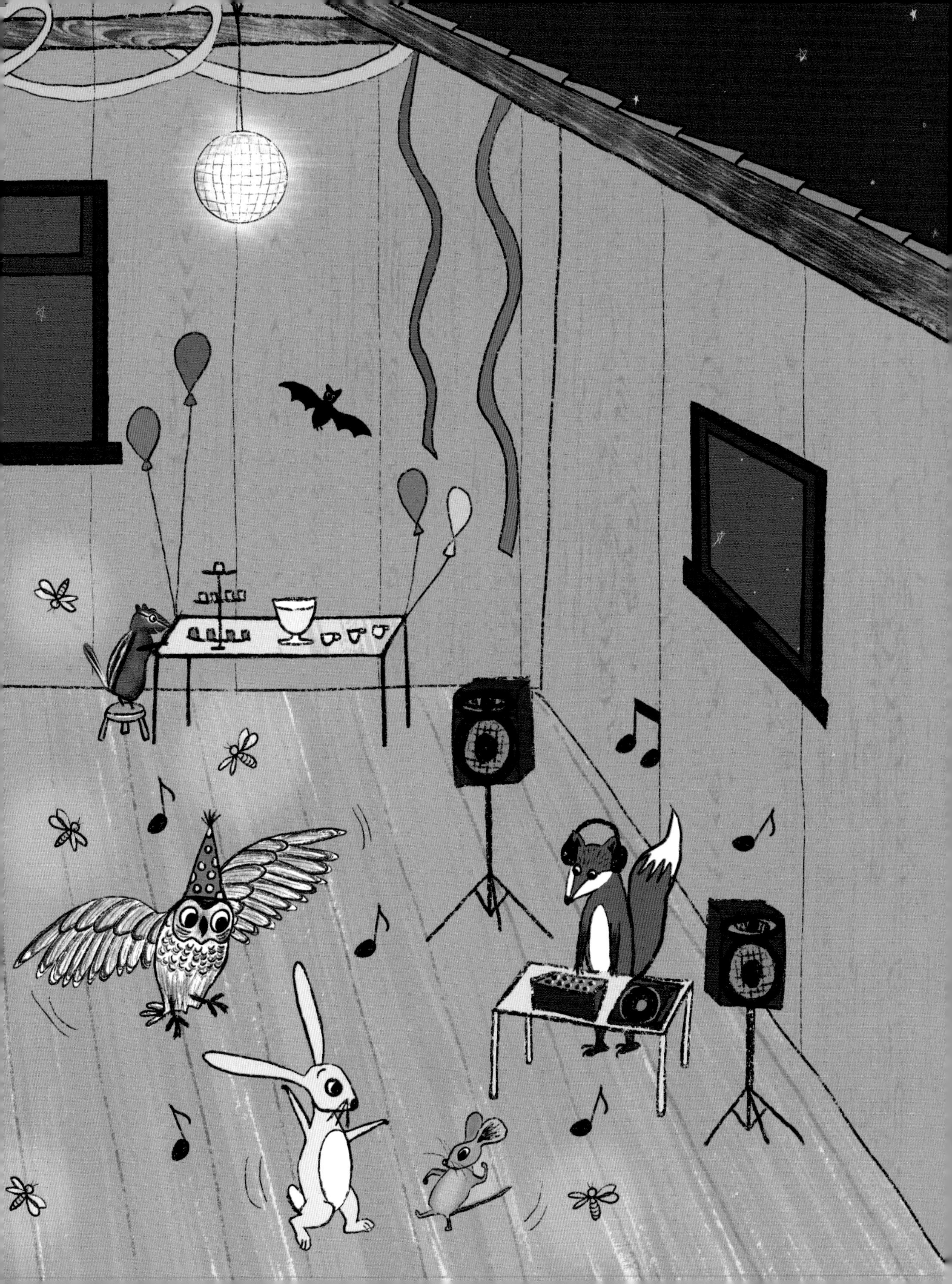

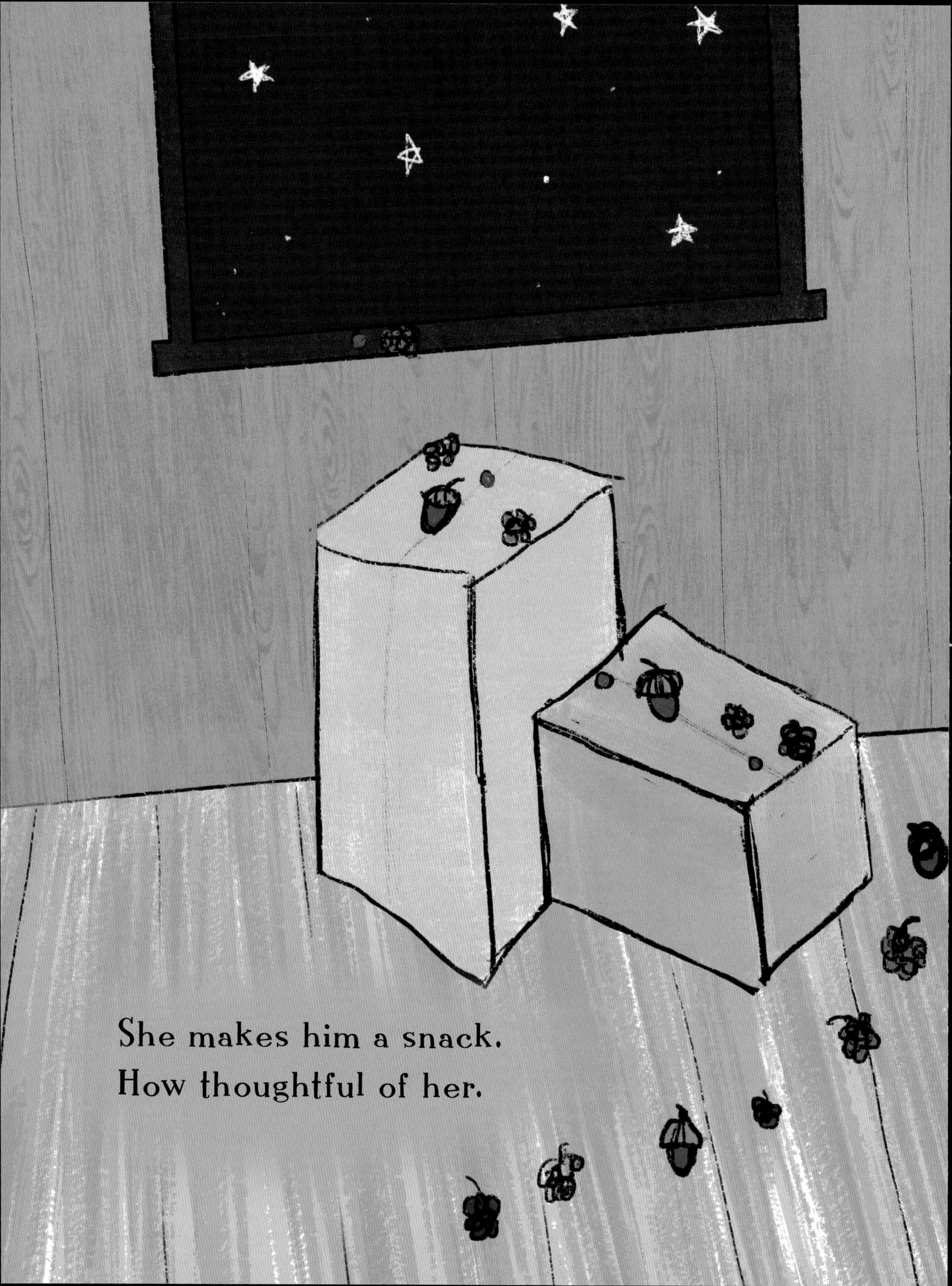

She makes him a snack.
How thoughtful of her.

Nellie puts away her slippers,

gets a drink
of water,

fluffs her pillows,

snuggles her bear,

and closes her eyes.
Finally.

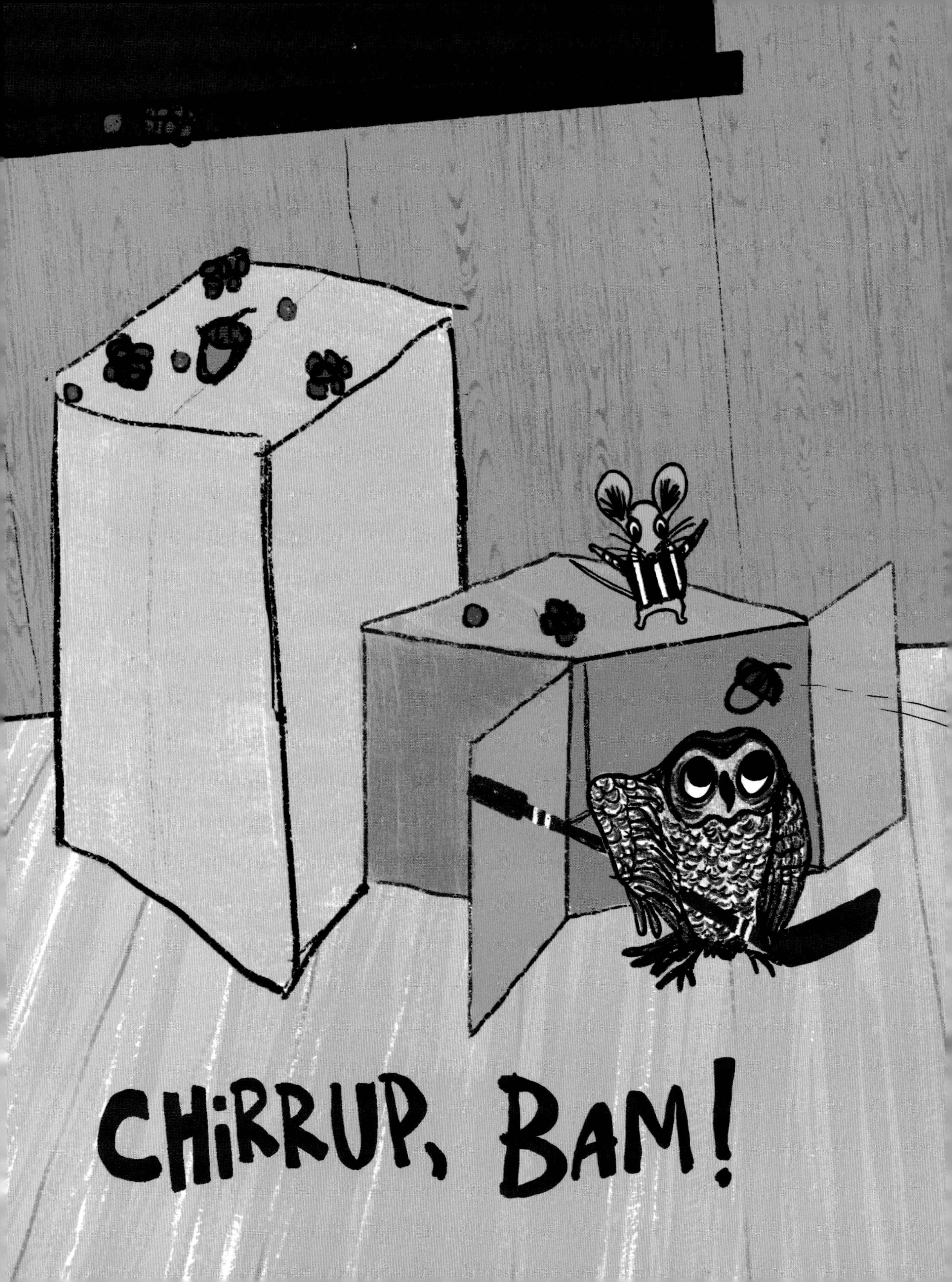
CHiRRUP, BAM!

SCRATCH, SLAP!
SQUEAK!

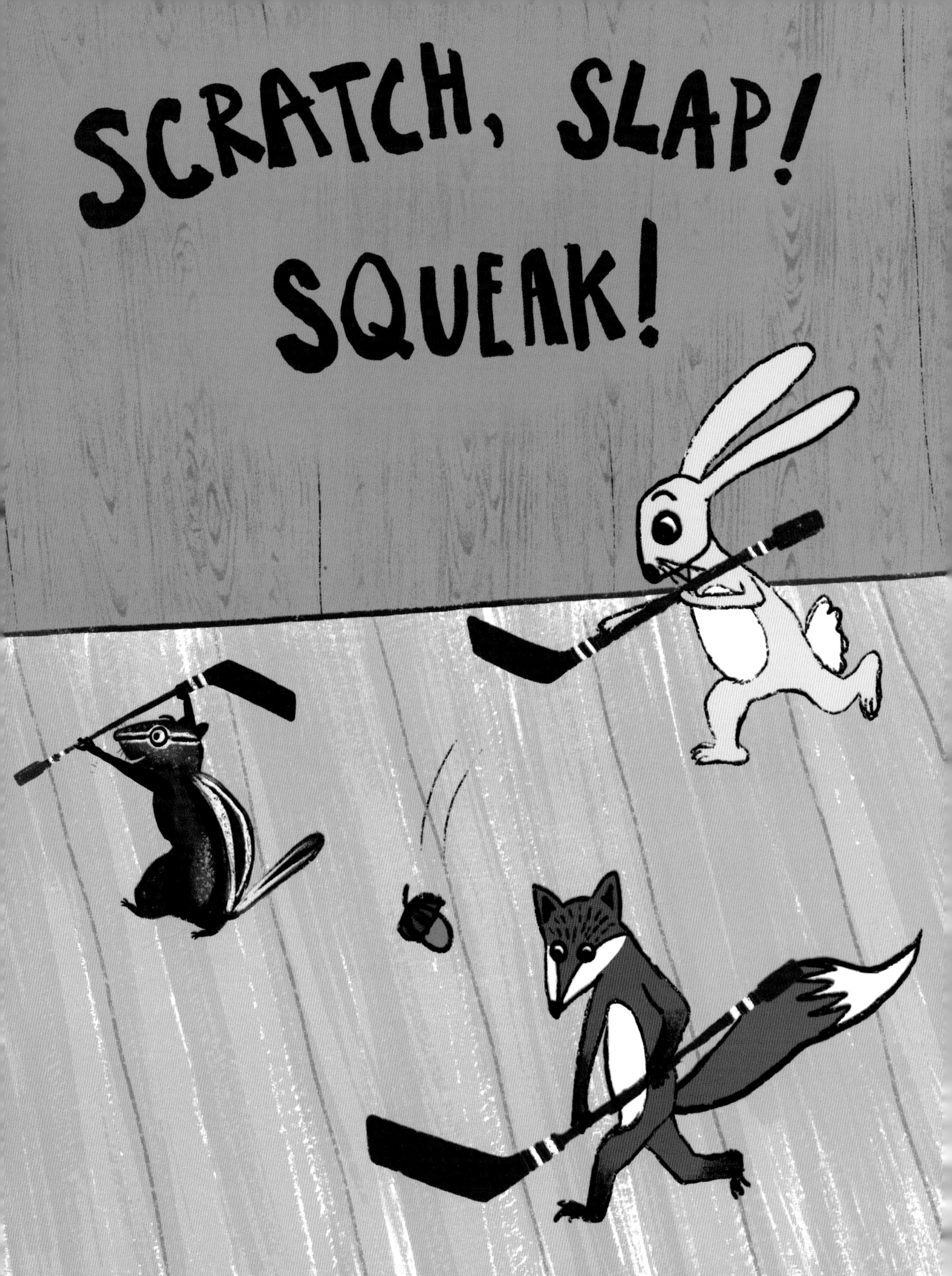

Nellie has had enough.

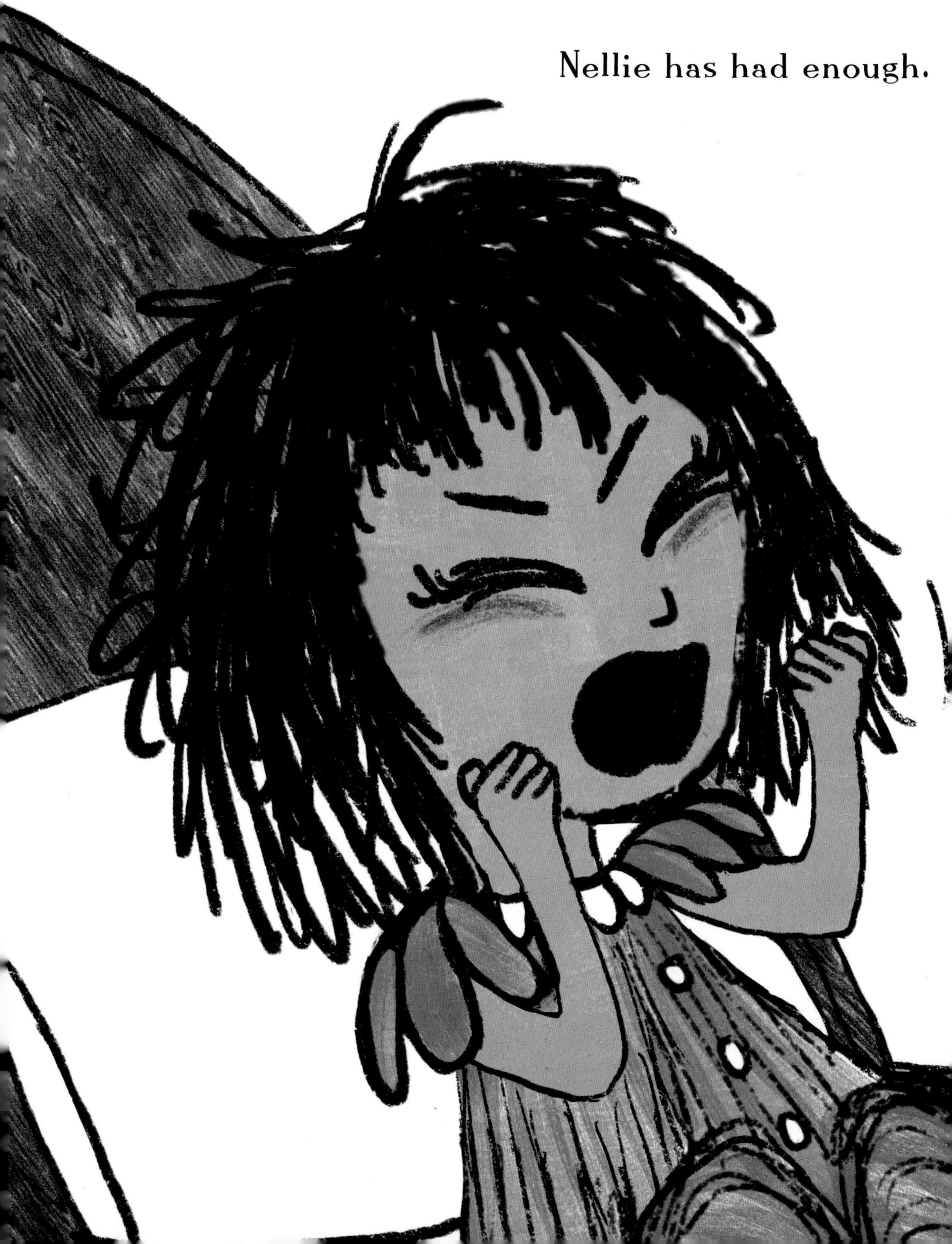

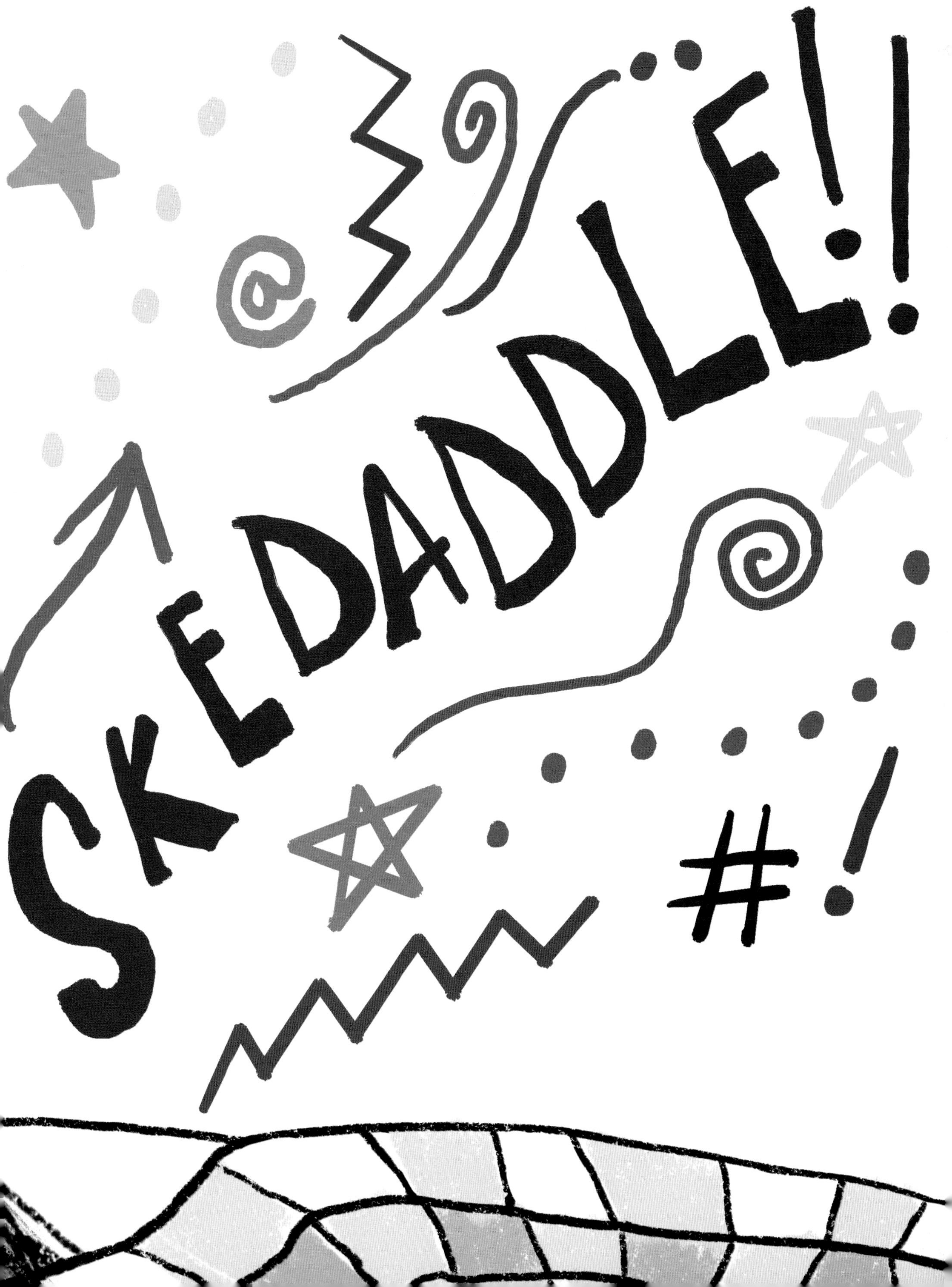
SKEDADDLE!!
#!

Yum Yum!

Ripe cheese will stink them out.

Ziggy will scare them out.

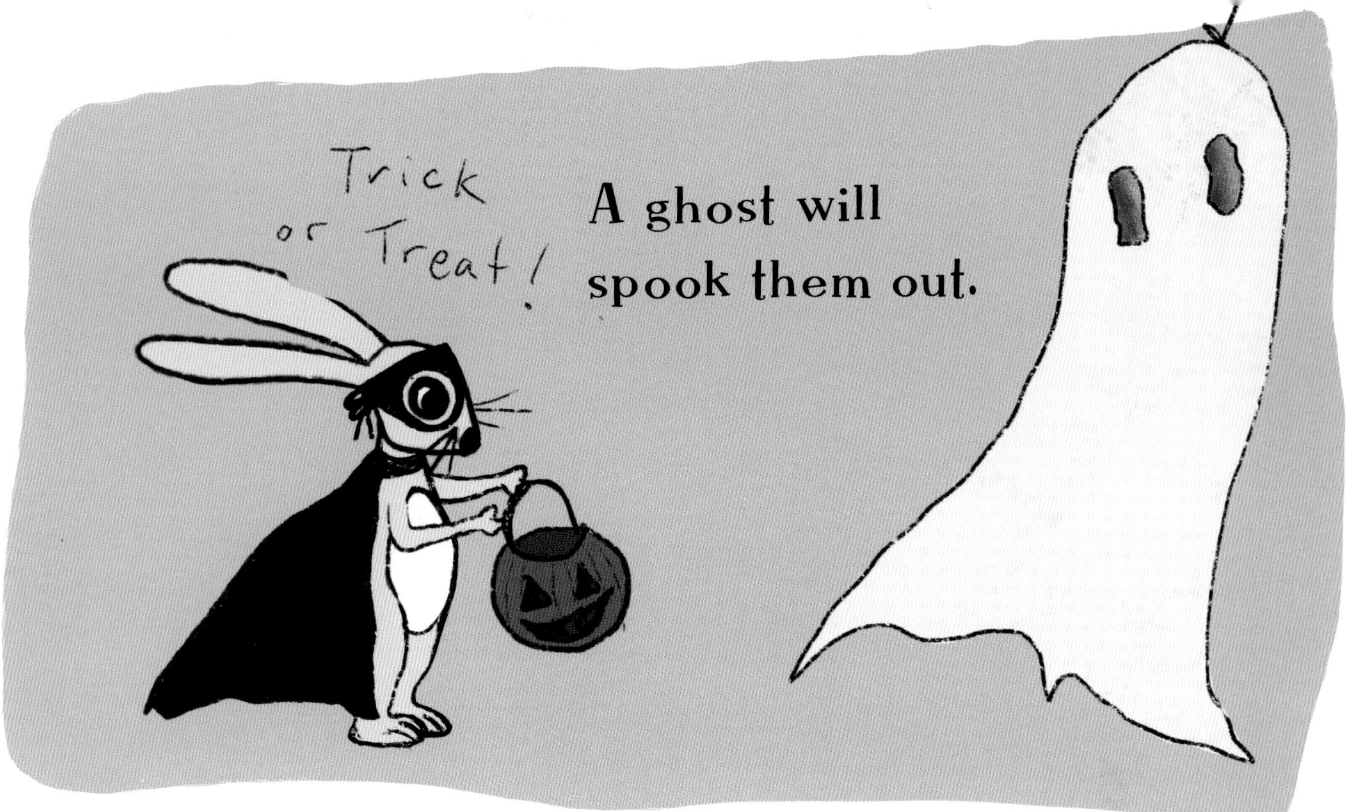
Trick or Treat!

A ghost will
spook them out.

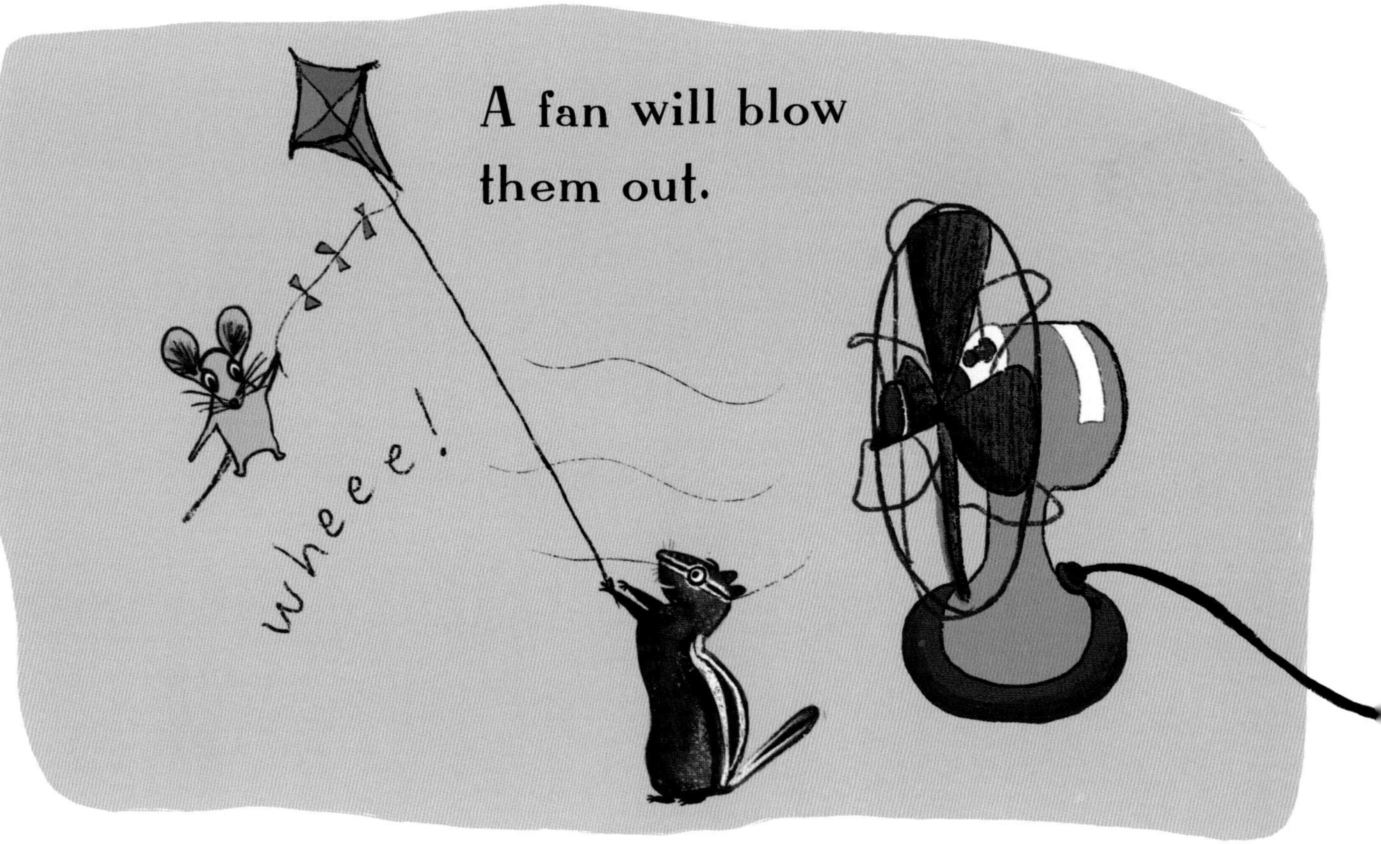
wheeee!

A fan will blow
them out.

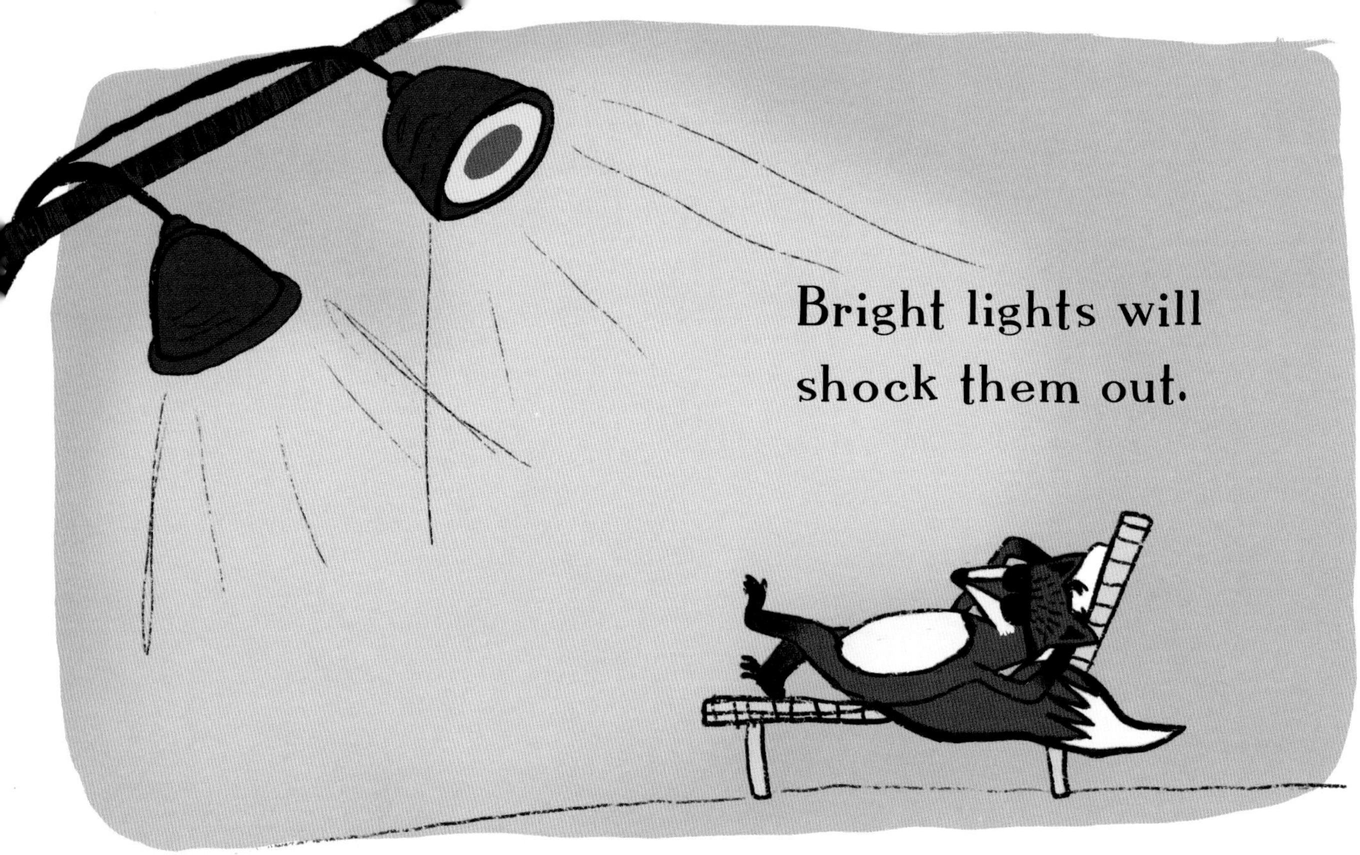

Bright lights will shock them out.

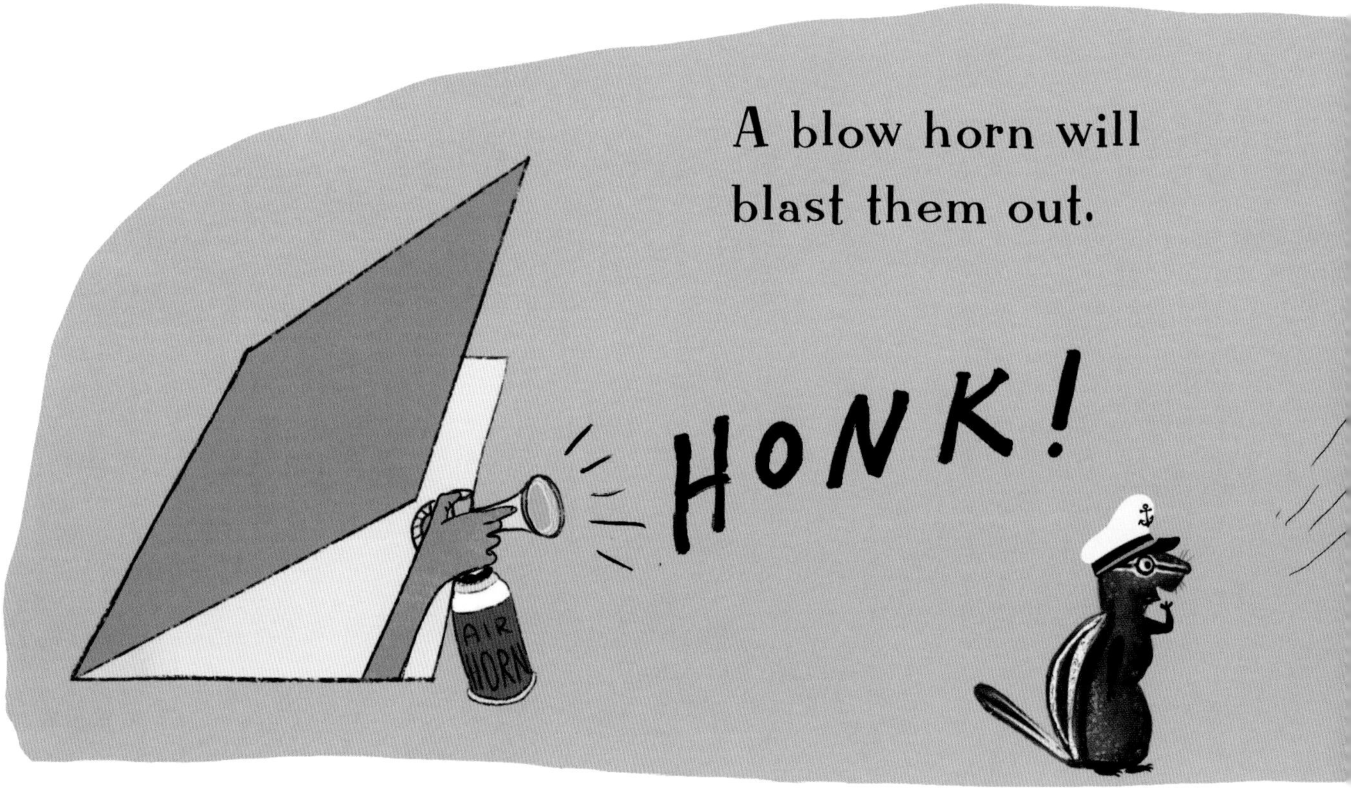
HONK!
AIR HORN

A blow horn will blast them out.

Animal Control will chase them out.

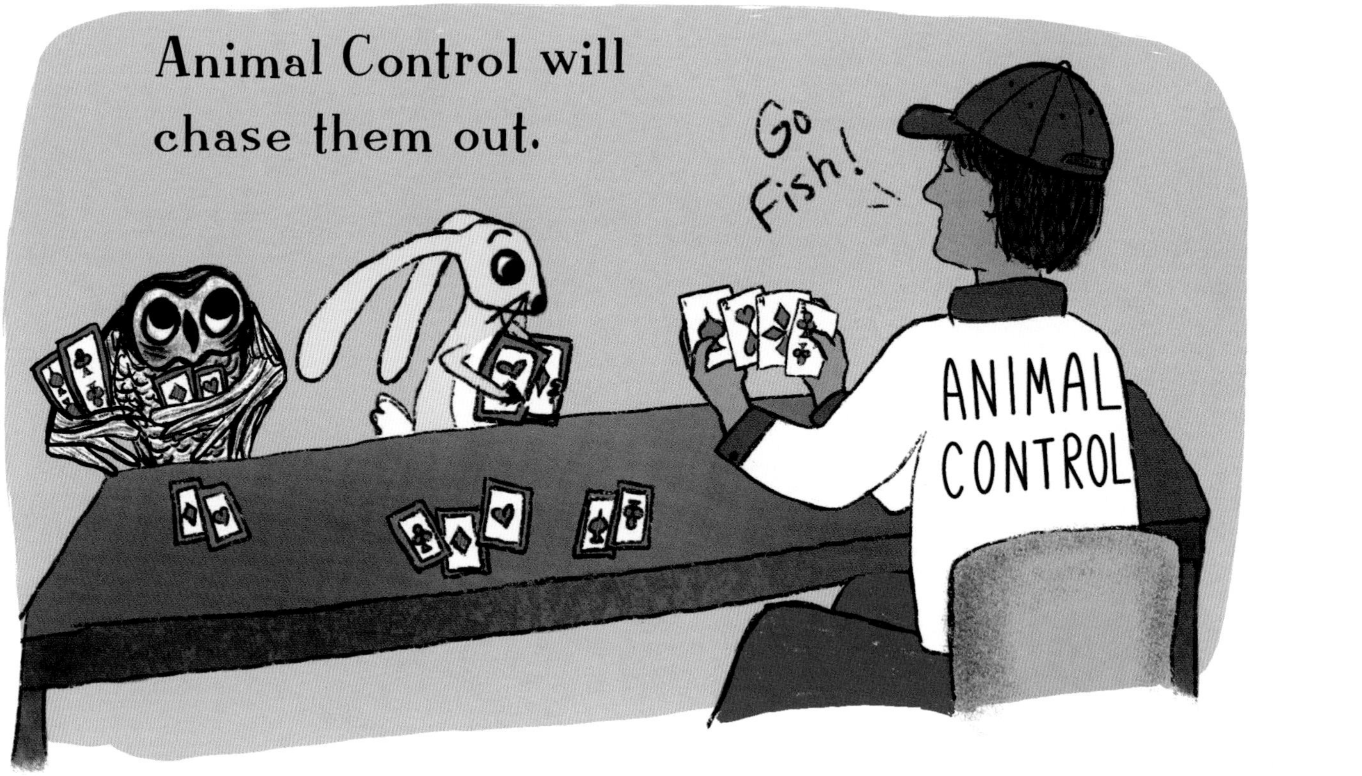
Go Fish!
ANIMAL CONTROL

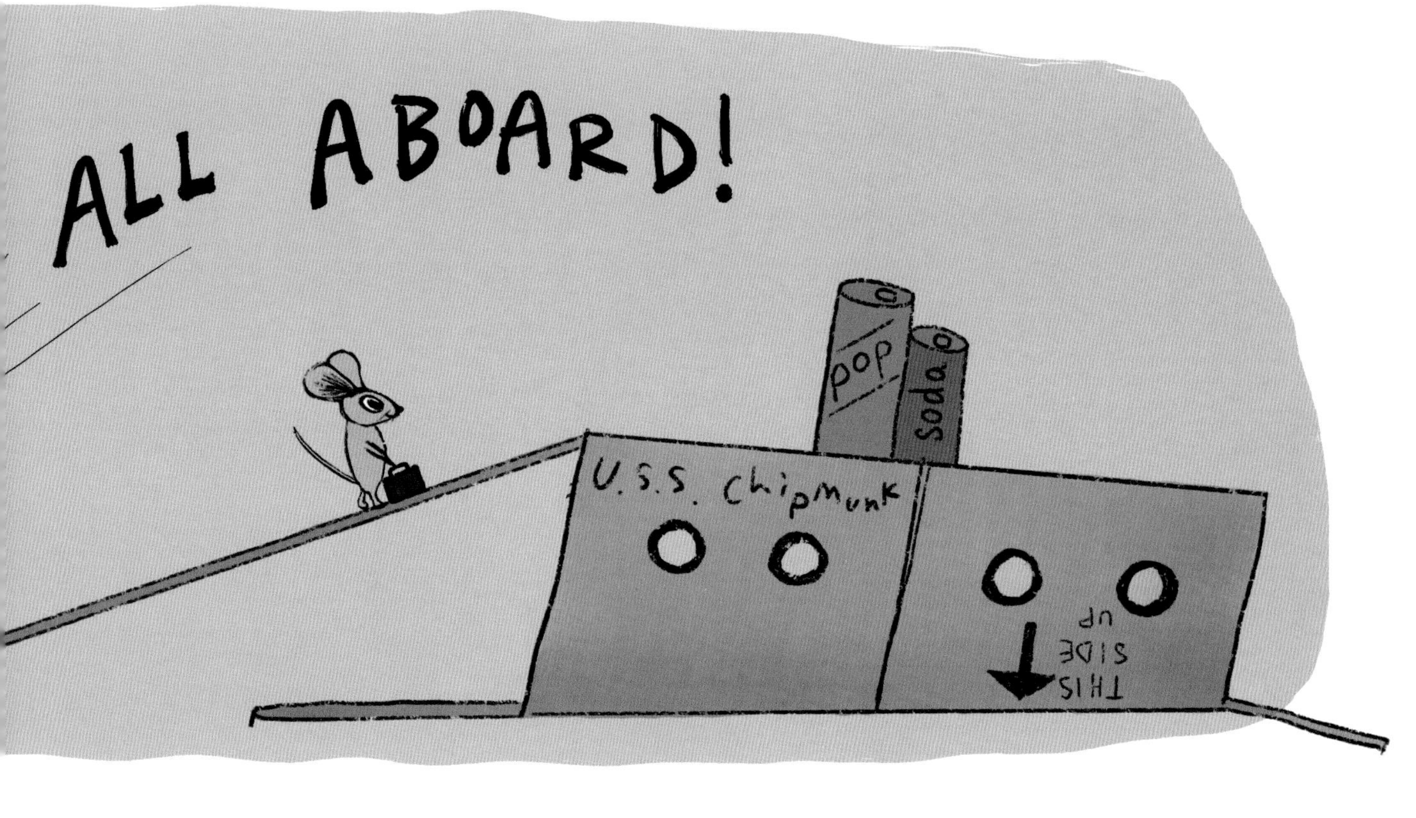
ALL ABOARD!
U.S.S. Chipmunk
pop
soda
THIS SIDE UP

Nellie has tried everything.

"Listen, chipmunk, I have got to get some sleep! Can you please keep it down?"

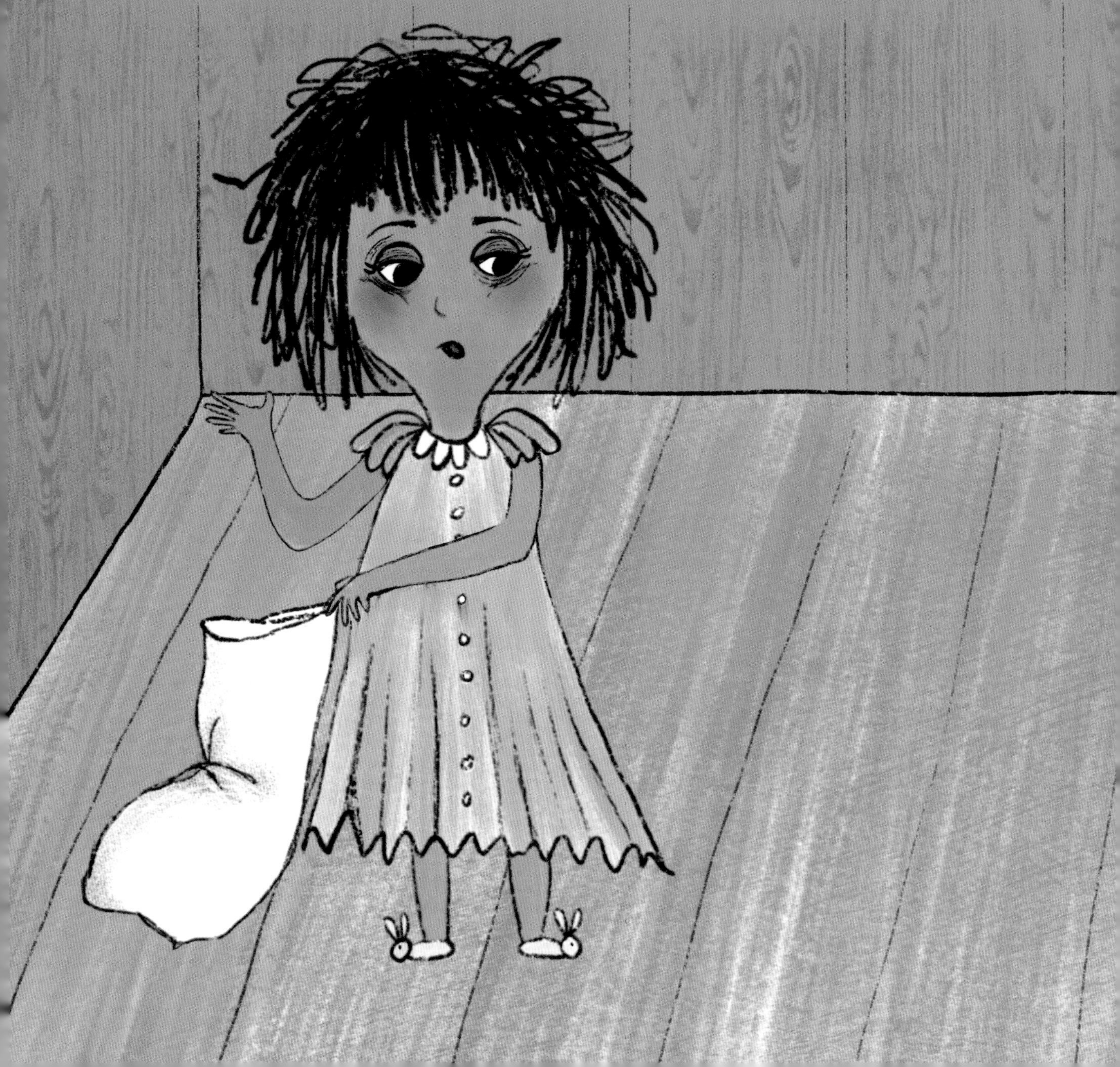

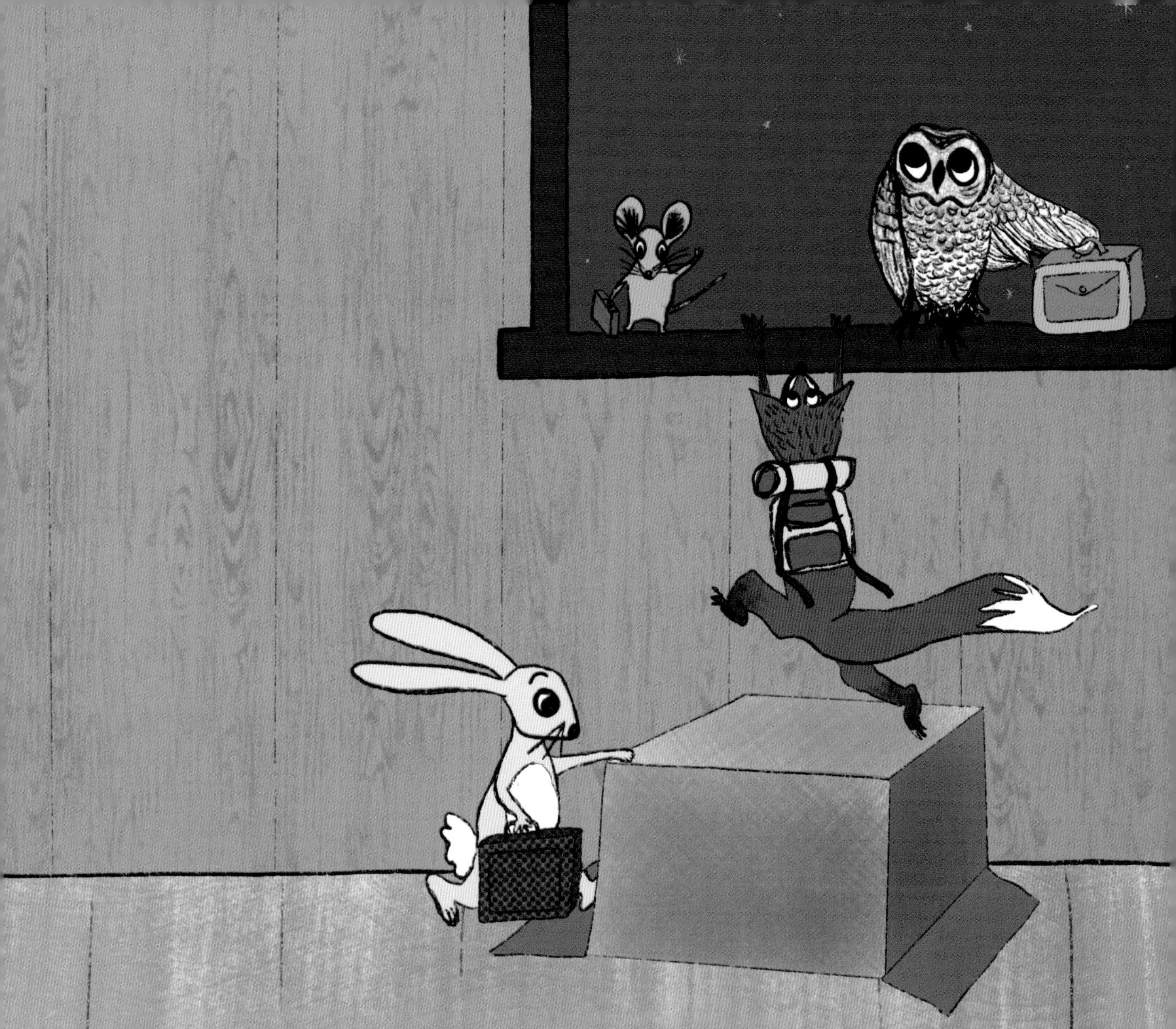

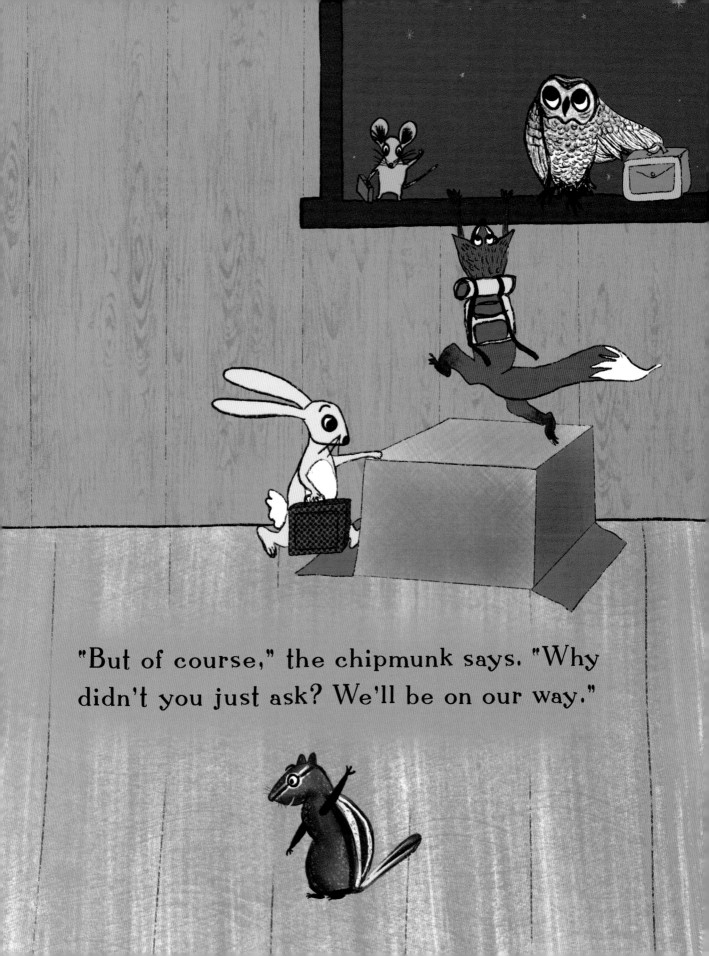

"But of course," the chipmunk says. "Why didn't you just ask? We'll be on our way."

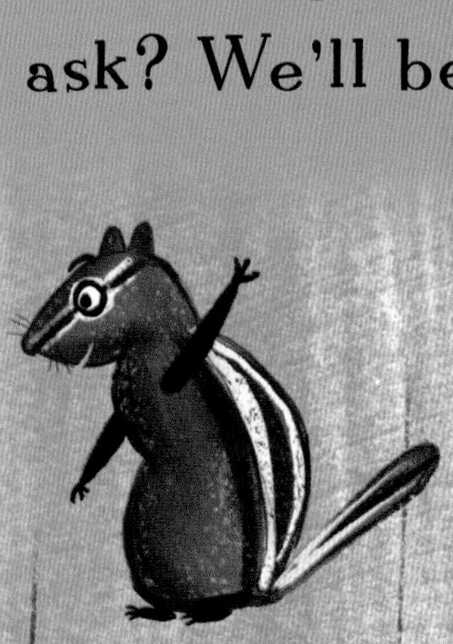

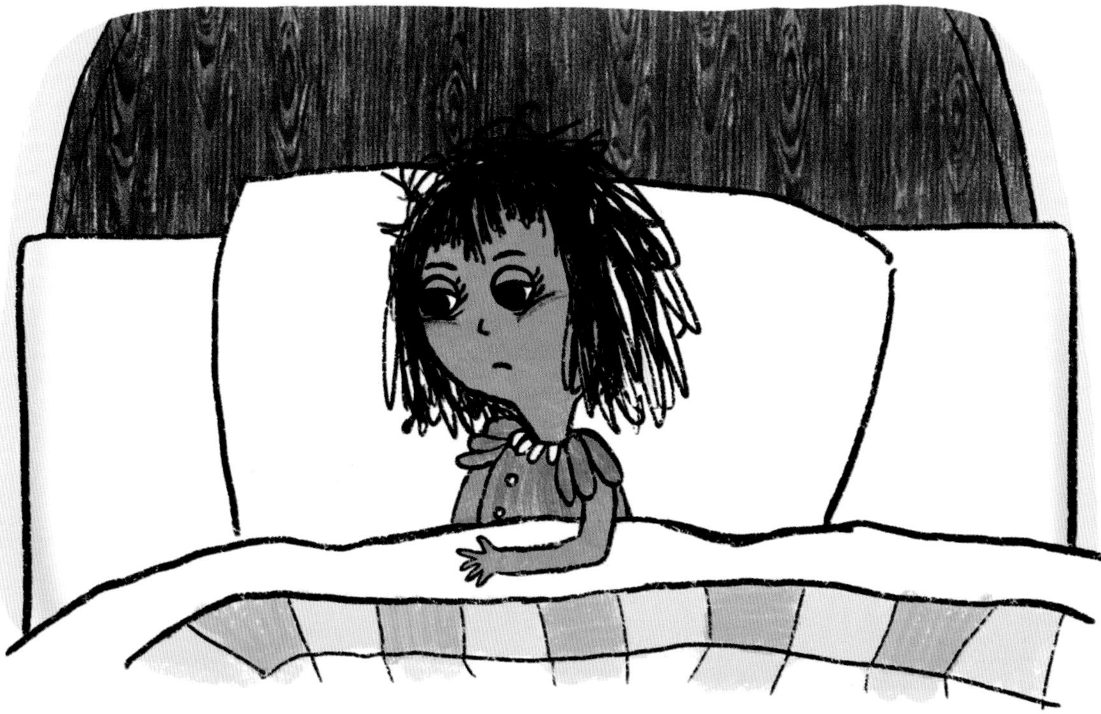

Nellie's room is finally silent.

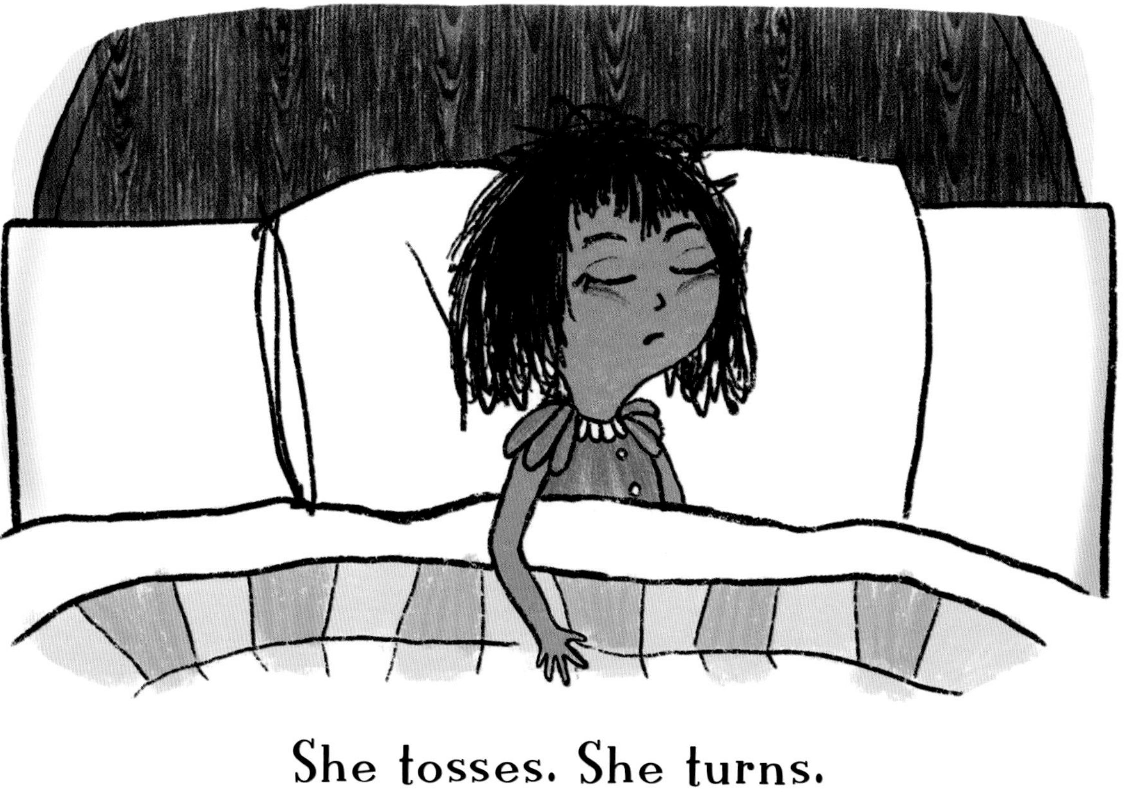

She tosses. She turns.

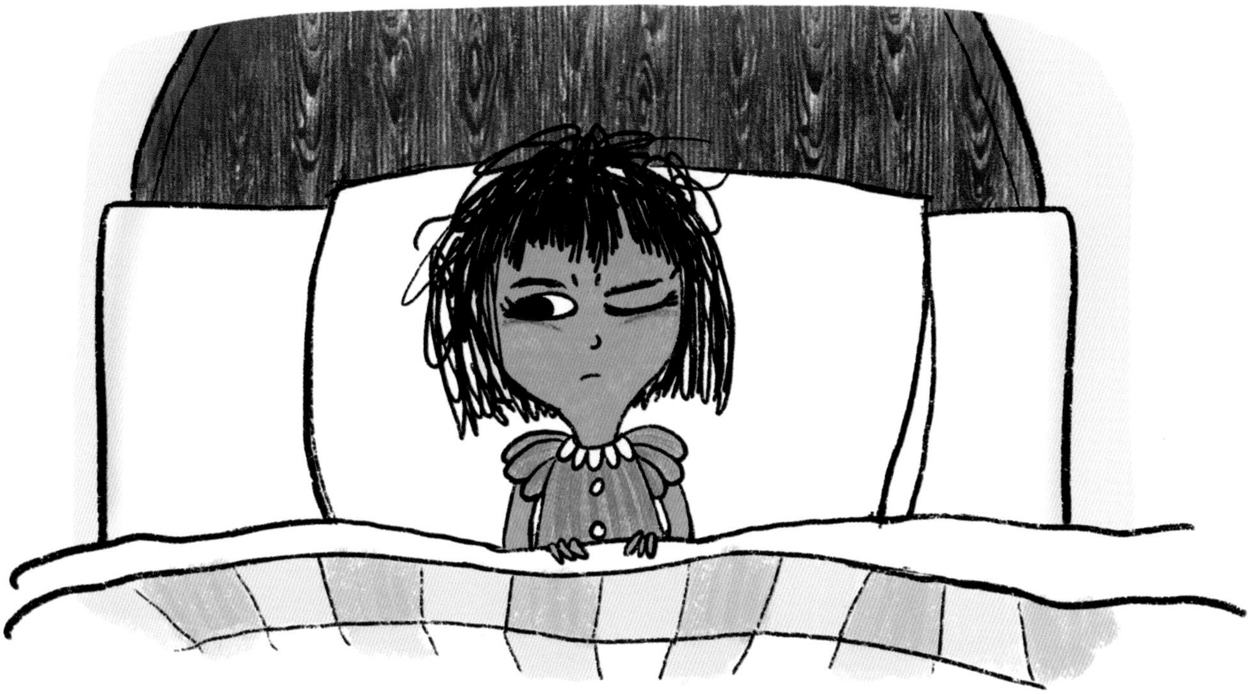

She cracks open one eye.

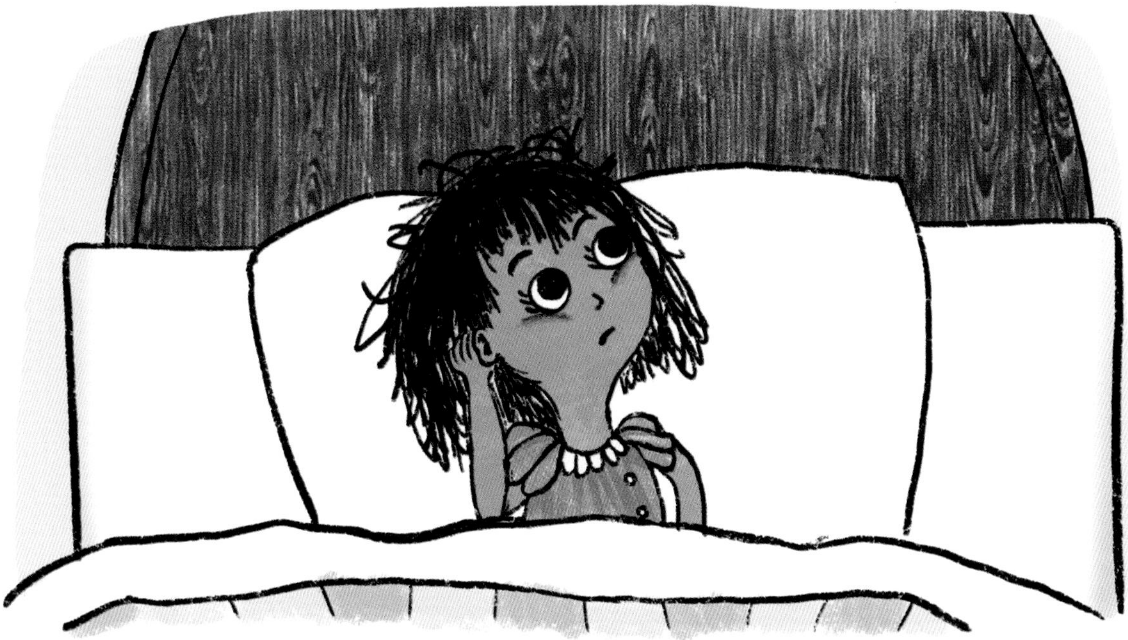

She listens to the quiet. No chirrup. No scratch.
And definitely no squeak.

But still Nellie can't sleep.

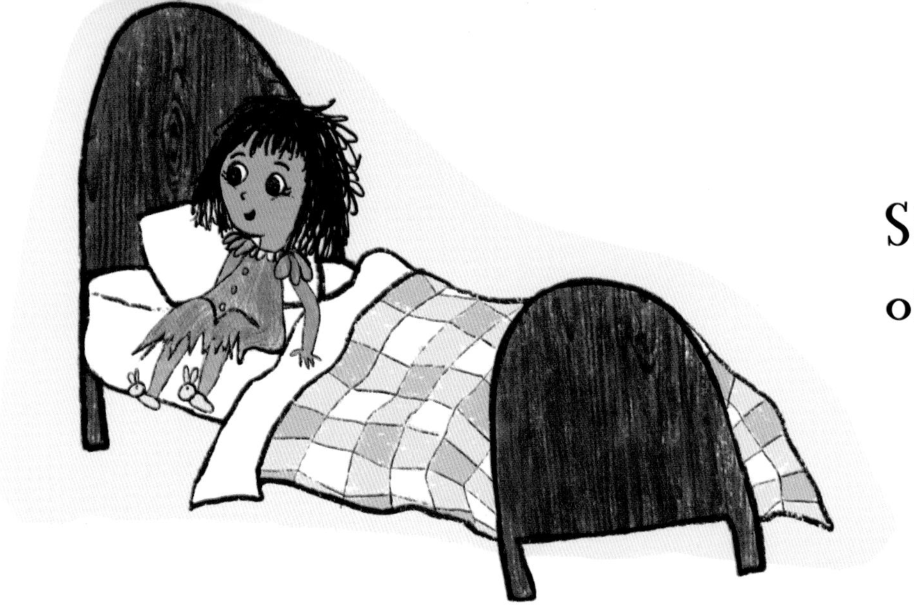

She hops out
of bed,

goes out to
the garden,

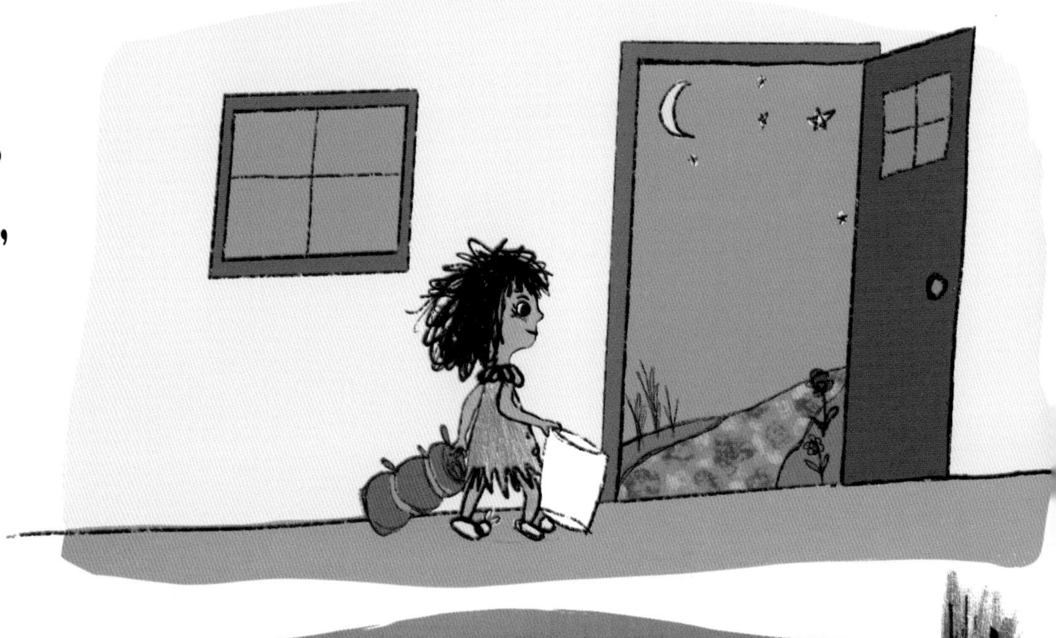

rolls out her
sleeping bag,

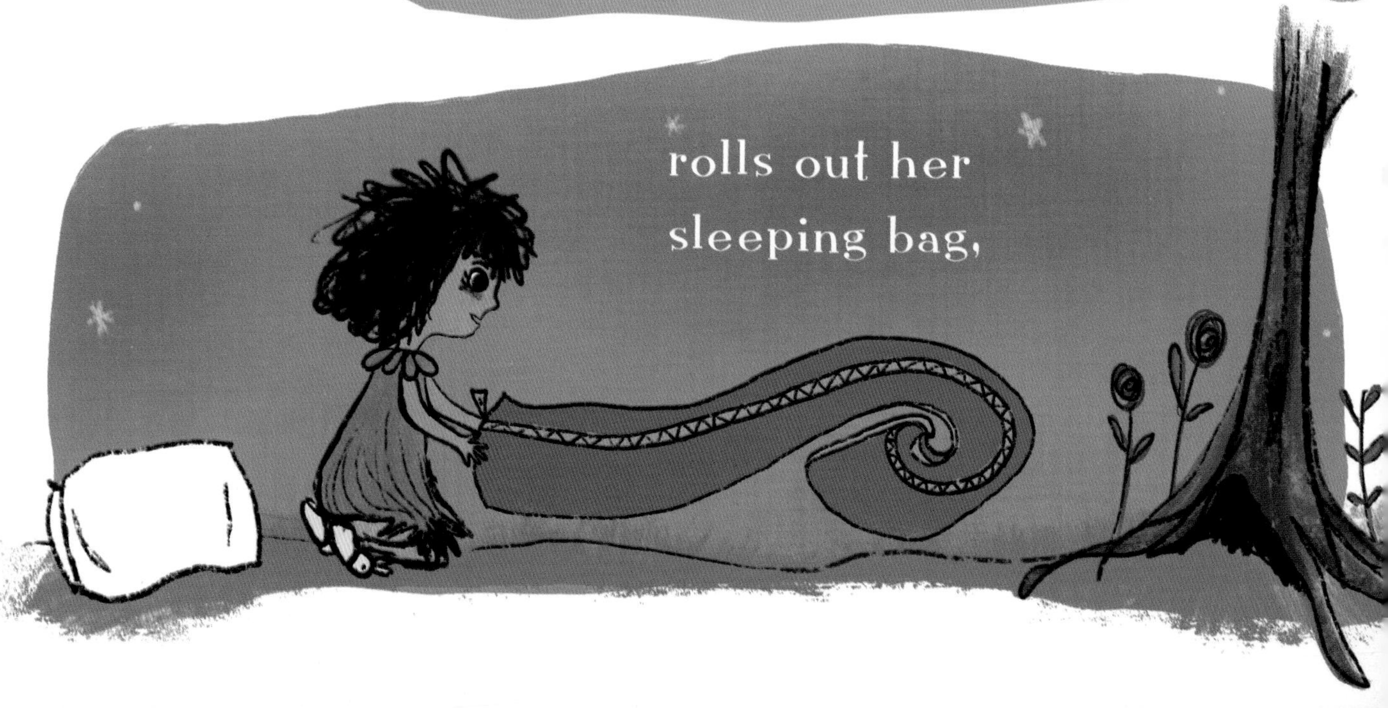

and closes her eyes.

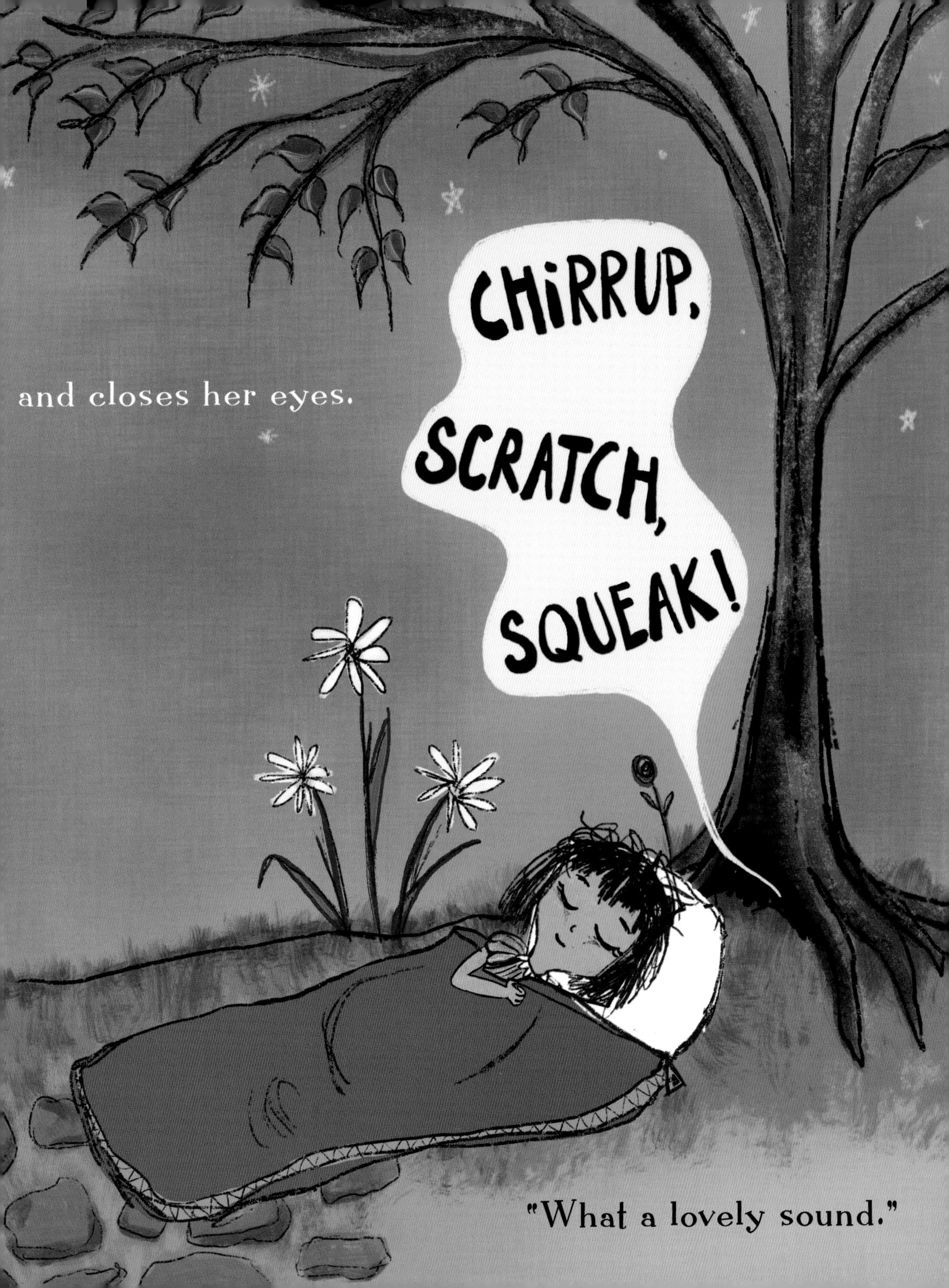
CHIRRUP,
SCRATCH,
SQUEAK!

"What a lovely sound."

One night, the chipmunk hears a strange noise above his head.

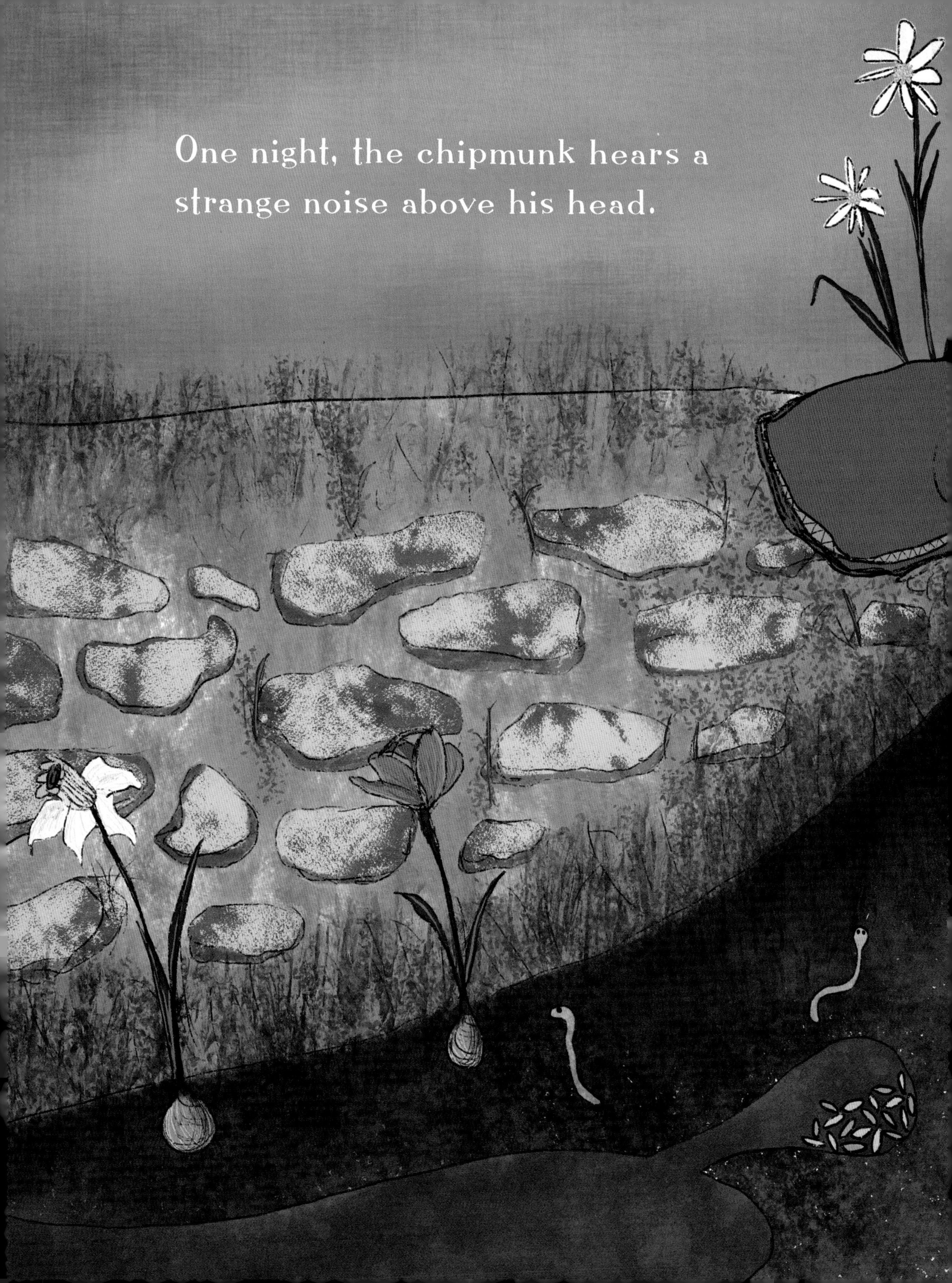

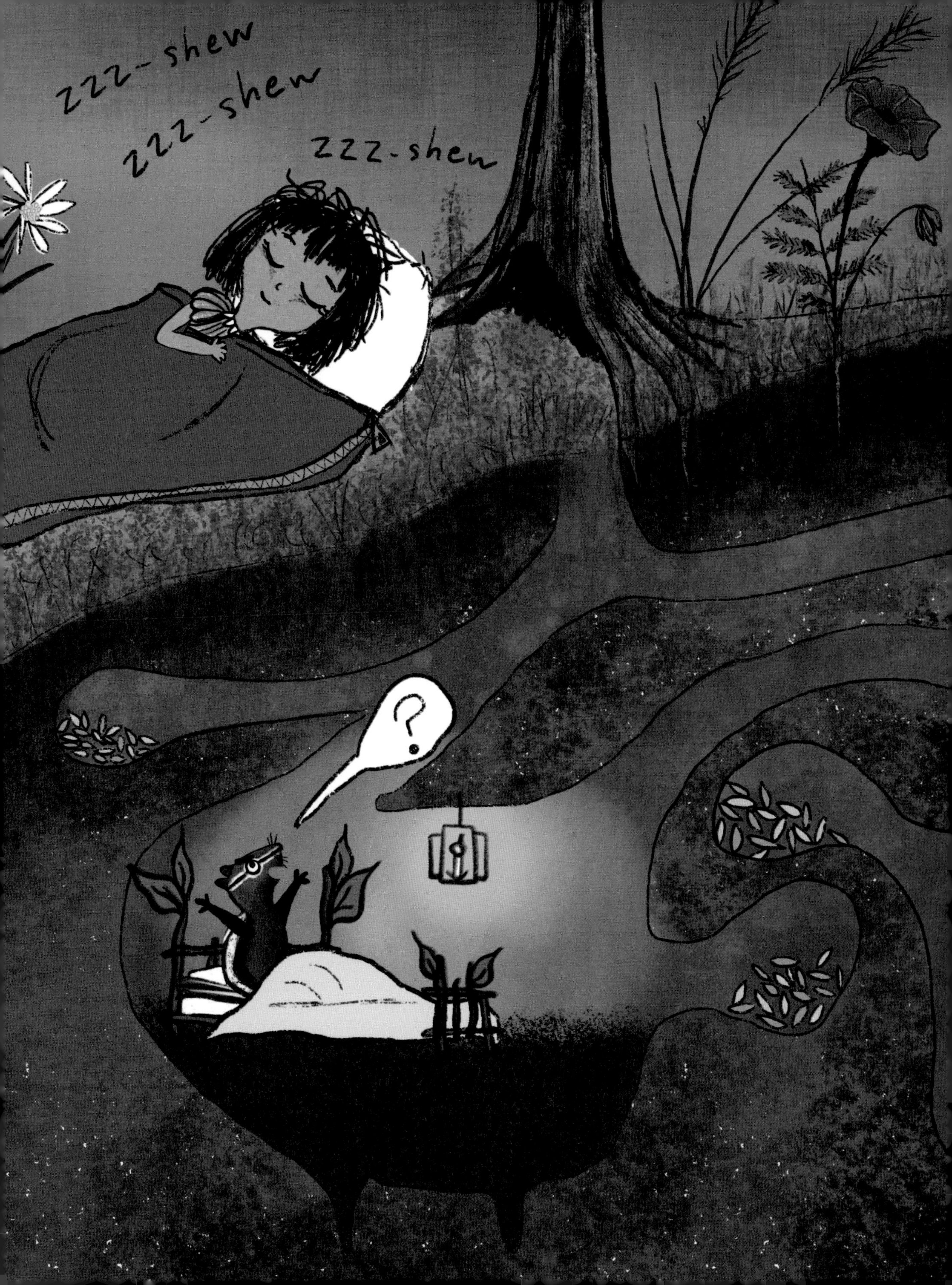
zzz-shew
zzz-shew
zzz-shew
?

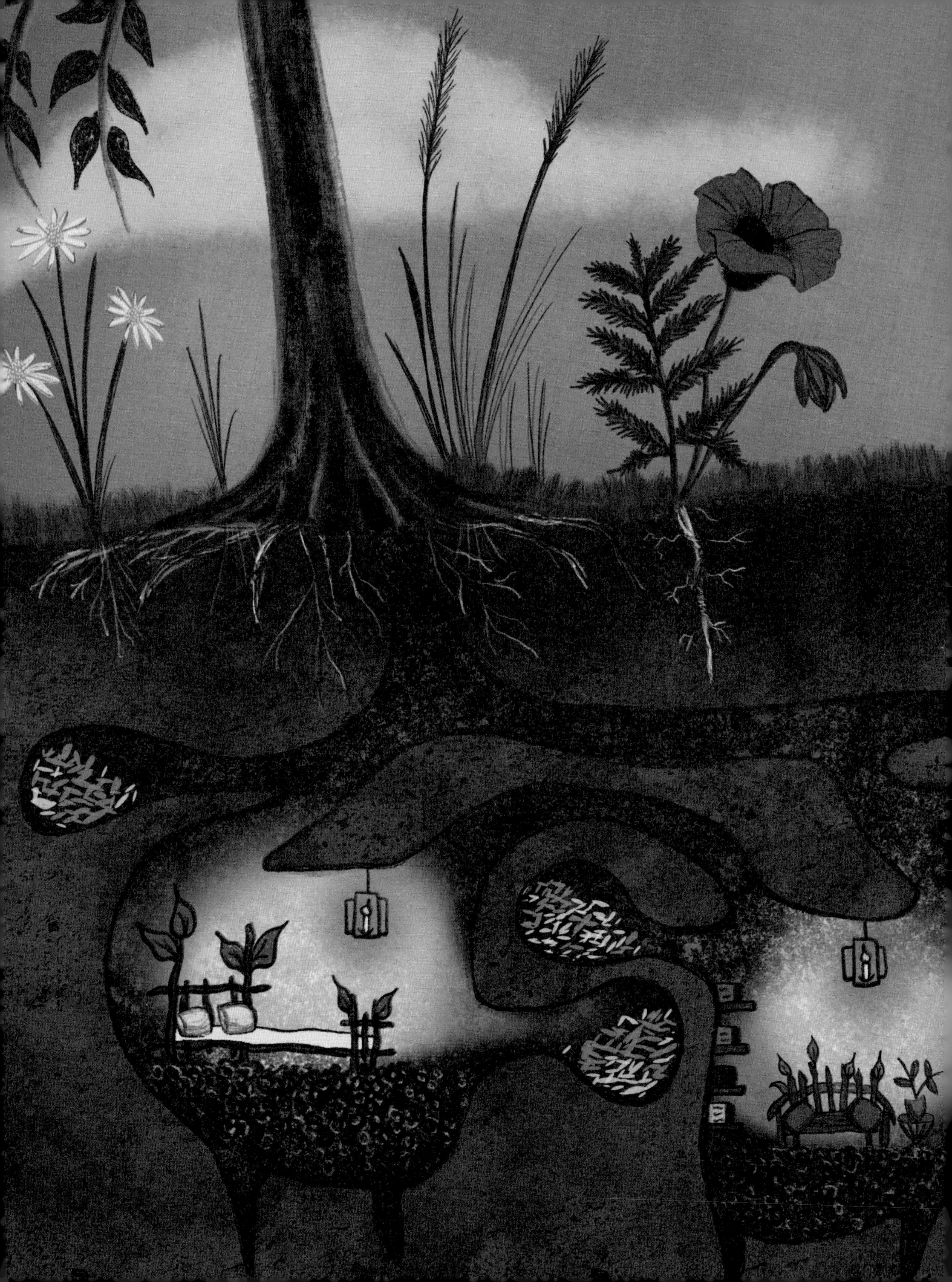